Return to Me

A Katama Bay Series

Katie Winters

Chapter One

From the forty-third floor of the Upper West Side high-rise apartment building, Janine Grimson Potter had a perfect view of Central Park. It was May 15th, and the glorious trees beyond had flourished with green foliage that beamed upward toward the eggshell-blue sky. That high up, the beeping chaos of traffic and the cries of angry New Yorkers didn't reach the ears. One was allowed to view the city as a miniature plaything, not a haven of millions of voices, opinions, backstories, and wild history. As Janine had spent her entire upbringing as one of the poorest New Yorkers, a Brooklynite, in fact, she felt her stance on the forty-third floor as though she'd ascended to heaven itself.

Her entire life had changed — approximately twenty-four years before. And she'd never looked back.

"Wow. That breeze is beautiful." Maxine Aubert stepped into the library and flashed a smile toward Janine. "You picked a perfect day for an engagement party."

Janine's heart fluttered as Maxine joined her at the window, which she'd cracked to allow the slightest breeze in. Janine held Maxine's eyes for a moment as Maxine squeezed her upper arm.

"You look like you're freaking out a little bit," Maxine finally said with a laugh.

Janine swept a dark lock of hair around her ear. "You know how it goes with these New York socialites. Trying to impress them has been my life mission for the past twenty years. But they always know that I'm not one of them."

"Well, mon cherie, neither am I," Maxine said. She dropped her head back so that her auburn hair flowed beautifully down her back. Her neck was reminiscent of a swan's. "But that's our great con, isn't it? We grew up in Brooklyn with nothing, and now, we've overtaken the kingdom."

"Just imagine if we told them the kinds of food we always ate as kids," Janine said. "Ramen noodles were a delicacy, along with the occasional KD entrée."

"I know. Imagine if they knew you hadn't tasted the likes of a soufflé until the age of twenty-five!"

Maggie Potter, Janine's eldest daughter, had recently gotten engaged to Rex Vanderson, a prestigious business-man, certainly a man from the upper echelon of Manhattan society. This sort of union required a high-caliber engagement party, and Janine had set to work on it immediately after news of their engagement had reached her ears. "Nothing but the best for my Maggie," had been her constant refrain as she had arranged everything.

Maggie's engagement party was set to begin at six thirty with a cocktail hour, followed by dinner, at one of the most prestigious and beautiful locations in Manhattan — the NoMad Hotel Rooftop. Now, it was just past five in the afternoon, and it seemed everything for the party had somehow fallen into place. This left Janine time to dress, have her makeup and hair done, and get over to the party.

Since Janine and Maxine had run around Brooklyn together in the '80s and '90s, there was very little that they didn't already know about each other. Now, as the light tipped toward sunset and expectation for the night ahead brewed in Janine's belly, they stripped down to their underwear and helped one another don their evening gowns. Janine's was dark blue, cut low over her breasts, and it hugged her hips beautifully.

"I'm glad I went on that low-carb diet when I did," she stated as she tilted herself sideways in the mirror. "I don't have your French genes, and I could tell that designer wasn't so sure about me when we first met."

Maxine buttoned the last of Janine's dress at the nape of her neck and made a funny sound in her throat. "You always look as sleek as any Parisian woman. The last time we were in Paris, I told you I heard many women whisper about your fashion sense. They were terribly envious."

Janine eyed her reflection in the floor-to-ceiling antique mirror, gifted to her for her thirty-fifth birthday by her husband, Jack. Behind her, Maxine upheld her high cheek-boned, French-woman looks, despite having moved to Brooklyn at the age of ten. Back when they'd been adolescents, prior to Janine meeting the ultra-rich Jack Potter, they hadn't needed anything or anybody.

"Why don't we open that champagne while we get ready?" Maxine suggested as she stepped toward her own dress, which hung in Janine's closet.

Tenderly, Maxine removed the champagne cork — a trick she'd taught Janine so that bubbles weren't flung across the room. She then poured them two flutes of champagne, lifted her glass, and said, "To the mother of the bride. You've worked yourself to death for this party, and I know it will go off without a hitch."

Janine blushed as she tinged her glass against Maxine's and sipped. "You're too kind to me."

"You know that we have to be honest in all things," Maxine told her. "I'll be the first to tell you when your fashion steps over the line."

"And you absolutely must tell me if I ever dress too young for my age," Janine said, her eyes widening. "That's my biggest fear. That I spot something Maggie or Alyssa are wearing and decide it will look good on me, too. I am not twenty anymore."

"And thank goodness for that," Maxine quipped. "I know we say it over and over again, but all the anxiety of our twenties? I wouldn't go back to that time for any amount of money."

The doorbell rang. Janine's housekeeper, who had busied herself preparing the apartment for the night's after-party, hustled for the door, then arrived at Janine's room to announce that the makeup and hair people were headed up. For the previous five years, Janine had used Chelsea and Connie, a twin-sister duo, for her hair and makeup. When they arrived, they greeted Maxine and Janine like old friends.

"This isn't just another Manhattan function," Connie said as she began to prepare Janine's curls so that they flourished beautifully down her shoulders. "This is your daughter's engagement party! You must be terribly excited."

"And terrified," Janine added. "You wouldn't believe the things these women will pick apart at parties like this. If you bring out the appetizers at inappropriate times, they'll chalk up the whole evening as a disaster."

Chelsea laughed uproariously. "Connie, I don't think we could ever hack this life."

"We never thought we'd be here, either," Maxine affirmed as Chelsea tied her hair into an intricate updo. "Just two Brooklyn girls with nothing to do but make trouble."

"That's right. I always forget. You girls are one of us," Connie said. Her tone remained slightly doubtful, as though she couldn't fully imagine the steps to take between her own life and the one Janine now enjoyed.

"You should have seen her when she met Jack," Maxine offered brightly, as she extended out her left hand and twirled her wrist so that her rings flashed in the soft light. "What was it you said, Janine? You said you'd met a man who'd changed everything."

"To be honest, I don't think he knew quite how poor I was," Janine said as a blush crept across her cheeks. "I was nineteen, waitressing, of course, and I just happened to stumble across a secondhand Chanel dress at a flea market that I wore for our first date."

"He didn't care what you wore," Maxine said with a funny arch of her eyebrow. "He just wanted to take it off you."

"Maxine!"

Connie and Chelsea erupted with laughter as Janine again eyed herself in the mirror. The conversation continued as Maxine explained her current dating life.

"I was married to a wealthy man myself," she said. "He died a few years ago and left me everything."

"Wow," Connie marveled. "You must miss him, though."

"She's definitely taught me a lot about the current dating scene in Manhattan," Janine replied. "I just love your stories, Max. You should tell the one about the baseball player."

"Oh, that darling twenty-five-year-old hunk of a man," Maxine chirped. "He never had a chance with me, but he sent me box tickets to his little games. With these men, I always play up the French thing. I even lather on the accent a bit more, you know, since I moved here when I was ten, and it really isn't so noticeable."

"It's just slightly there. Like a hint of the music of the French language," Chelsea affirmed.

"But these men. They must fall head over heels!" Connie cried.

Maxine chuckled. "I have to admit that I'm having a terrific time. Even at forty-three years old."

"And you're not slowing down yet," Janine said.

"I'll drag you out on the town with me one of these days," Maxine warned. "Now that Maggie's engaged, and Alyssa's been out of the house for a few years, it's time to inject some life into your Manhattan nights."

"Jack and I are so settled, and you know I like that about my life," Janine said, as her heart swelled slightly. "He's been so busy with work for the past year or so, but he promised he would calm down soon so that we can travel more and spend more time together."

"It's the secret to a happy marriage," Chelsea affirmed. "My husband and I make sure we have a date night once a week. Sometimes I get so excited about it, especially if I haven't seen him for a while. I'll dress up, do my hair, that sort of thing."

"It's so important," Janine agreed. "It's not that I don't respect Jack's career. I do. He's killed himself for it. But we fell in love for a reason. And I want to remind him that we have a beautiful future ahead of ourselves — into our forties and our fifties and our sixties."

"That's beautiful," Connie and Chelsea said in unison.

When Janine and Maxine finished their looks for the night, they sipped a final glass of champagne and bid goodbye to Connie and Chelsea, who they called "masters."

"Thank you for helping us middle-aged women look a little less ragged." Janine chuckled.

"As if you need any real help with that," Chelsea said.

When the girls had gone, Janine and Maxine stepped into the kitchen to check on the staff. They had just begun to arrive to prepare for the after-party drinks and cuisine. Janine ironed out the details while Maxine checked her phone. Then Janine texted her daughters and her husband to make sure everyone was headed to the NoMad Hotel rooftop.

> MAGGIE: Already here, Mom! Alyssa just got here, too.

> JACK: On my way.

Janine sent heart emojis to all three of her favorite people, her dear family, and then turned her eyes toward Maxine. Throughout their incredibly long friendship, Maxine had never once spoken about having children herself. But each time Janine acknowledged the enormous mountain of love she had for her daughters, she wondered if Maxine stirred in any amount of jealousy.

"What do you think, Max? You ready?"

Maxine's eyes sparkled. "As ready as I'll ever be to face those monster socialites."

"Just remember that being in their midst means we won," Janine said with a slight smile.

"If we could only turn back the clock and watch the event from that point of view," Maxine said. "We would have gawked at the cost of all this. No, we would have thought ourselves to be insane."

"Ridiculous, isn't it?" Janine said as she swept her hair behind her shoulders.

Maxine reached out to grip Janine's shoulder. Her lips curved into an O. "Wow. Janine, you look absolutely breathtaking. I just want you to know that."

Janine's grin was enormous, the kind she tried to avoid these days so as not to wrinkle up her face. "So do you, Max. So do you."

"Why do we even care about compliments from men?" Maxine asked as they clacked in their heels toward the closet to gather their coats. "All we should appreciate are kind words from women. It's not as though any man I flirt with tonight will notice the fine detail of my eyeliner or the beautiful intricacies of your curls."

"You're exactly right," Janine said as she brought her coat over her shoulders. "Jack will probably say something like, 'Nice dress, babe,' then carry on whatever conversation he's in."

Maxine's laugh was uproarious. "Men. Who needs them?"

"We really should have just married one another when we had the chance," Janine jested. "How happy we would be!"

Chapter Two

Janine's driver stopped the car at the corner of Broadway and idled as several taxis whizzed around them, their drivers honking their horns. Janine and Maxine gathered their purses and eyed the various partygoers as they scuttled from their taxis and headed toward the hotel's entrance. There was Marcia Collingsworth, who'd married a rich newspaperman only a few years prior to his death, and had spent the majority of the next decade sleeping with as many of his rich friends as she could; then, there were several of Jack's business associates and dear childhood friends, all of whom had more money than God.

"Oh, good. There's Alyssa," Janine said as her driver opened the door and helped her out onto the curb.

"Wow. That dress she has on!" Maxine said approvingly, just as Alyssa whipped around, allowing her lavender gown to sweep in a beautiful parabola just above her ankles.

Alyssa was twenty-two years old and, just a week before, had walked across the stage as a Yale graduate.

She was a beautiful creature, nearly a twin to Maggie, with dark tresses that curled beautifully down her back and a perfect figure. Maxine often reminded Janine that her daughters were the spitting image of their mother, which was definitely true, even as it grew more and more difficult for Janine to remember herself like that.

"Mom!" Alyssa cried. She rushed toward her, bringing along a wave of perfume, then dotted a kiss on her mother's cheek. "You look absolutely stunning. As do you, Maxine."

"There she is. The Yale graduate." Maxine beamed. In Janine's eyes, Maxine had been a kind of stand-in aunt for the girls over the years. She had even gone so far as to take Alyssa out for her twenty-first birthday the previous year when Janine had been sick with the flu. "I'm terribly sorry I missed the ceremony."

"Oh, it was as boring as ever," Alyssa said as she whipped a hand back and forth. "Just a bunch of caps, gowns, and bad speeches."

"Your mom and I never graduated from college, so these achievements are impressive, kiddo," Maxine said as she gave Janine a side-eyed glance.

Maxine had frequently told Janine over the years to remind her daughters just how far she'd come — that her background hadn't supplied her every opportunity in the world. Maggie and Alyssa were set for life, as though they'd been born Manhattan royalty.

"I know that," Alyssa said softly. "I count my blessings every day for my education."

"Let's get inside, shall we?" Janine said as she squeezed her best friend's hand in thanks. "After all this planning, I think it's finally time to enjoy ourselves."

They entered the swanky hotel, were greeted with

importance, and ushered upstairs. Once on the rooftop, Janine feasted her eyes on the beautiful view before her—the perfect décor of the long tables, the large floor candles, and fairy lights that hung everywhere—giving the room a certain ambiance. The gorgeous Manhattan guests were dressed to the nines, and they all stood around with cocktails in their hands, eating small snacks and speaking to one another earnestly as though they cared what the other said. Everything seemed picture-perfect, cut straight out of a magazine, and Janine knew, someday soon, this very view of her party would stretch across the pages of many magazines. When the Potters threw parties in Manhattan, the world knew about them.

This was all thanks to her immaculate party-planning capabilities. She was quite proud, to say the least.

"Darling!" One of her friends, Gwyneth, stepped out from another conversation. She was a petite little thing, and her designer-made dress hung from her like strange curtains. She stepped toward Janine with big doe eyes and a fake smile as she cried, "This is really just so splendid, isn't it? Oh, Maxine, you'll have to help me. What is it the French would call something like this? Encroyable?"

Maxine seemed on the verge of rolling her eyes yet stopped herself at the last moment. "Perhaps we'd say 'relou.'"

"Relou..." Gwyneth formed the word across her tongue and furrowed her brow. "It really is such a beautiful language, isn't it?"

Janine made a mental note to ask Maxine what that actually meant in French as Gwyneth began to pepper her with information regarding her own daughter and her recent graduation from Princeton. In the meantime,

Alyssa stepped away to find the bride, who it seemed, was located toward the far end of the rooftop, with Rex's arm flung around her lower back. Maggie seemed to be in the middle of telling an elaborate story; Janine could just sense it, the way her eldest daughter's eyes sparkled.

"I hope you don't mind, Gwyneth, but I must go say hello to the bride-to-be," Janine finally said as she gripped Gwyneth's hands and tilted herself toward Maggie and Alyssa. "I hope we'll have more time to speak later?"

By the time she freed herself from Gwyneth, a few more lurkers had latched onto her. After several minutes more, Janine was able to kick off her Manhattan guests, and she pressed herself through the crowd to find her darling daughter. Maggie's eyes widened when she spotted her mother. She rushed toward her, wrapping herself in a hug with Janine, knowing full well that wasn't the kind of thing you did at functions like this.

"Mom." Maggie pulled away and said under her breath, "This party is spectacular. You really outdid yourself this time. Thank you so much."

Janine blushed only slightly. "Darling, my eldest only gets married once."

Maggie laughed as she flipped her hair in that very same way she always had as a little girl. "Let's hope so, at least, huh?"

"Come now. I've never met a happier couple than you and Rex," Janine said.

Maggie's eyes traced over Janine's shoulder. She paused for a moment and swirled her drink. "Maxine didn't bring a date? I told her she could."

"She said she couldn't find anyone," Janine replied. "But you know Maxine. She's always fine to be by herself.

She always has been. I have to say, she's a whole lot stronger than me."

At that moment, Maggie yanked her head around, and her jaw dropped as a large bouquet of red roses burst into her arms. "Daddy!" she cried as Jack Potter himself, a man who always liked to make an entrance, wrapped her in a hug.

The girls had always loved their father, no matter how many business trips he took, no matter how much it seemed that his career took first place over his family. Janine was grateful that the great Jack Potter managed to juggle everything at once.

When their hug broke, Jack turned and looked at Janine eagerly. "How about this, Janny?" This was a silly nickname he'd tried to make work for years. "Rooftop of NoMad? You really went above and beyond. This is fantastic!"

"Is that a silly dad pun?" Maggie cried.

"You bet it is," Jack said as he waggled his eyebrows. "Just because my little girls are both grown up doesn't mean I'll ever stop being a dad."

Jack stepped away to speak to a colleague of his, which left Maggie and Janine. Maggie was just the slightest bit taller than her mother, especially in the heels she now wore, which they had purchased together on a mother-daughter trip to London the previous month.

"Rex looks freaked out, doesn't he?" Maggie whispered.

Janine eyed her fiancé, who looked dashing in his Italian-cut suit. He spoke with his hands as though everything filled him with passion.

"He's over-compensating," Maggie explained. "He hates to have all the attention on him."

"I understand," Janine offered. "When your father and I had our engagement party, I was pregnant, and the conversation wasn't so bright and optimistic. Plus, you know— I was this girl from the other side of the tracks."

Maggie shook her head. "I really can't imagine that. Grandma and Grandpa must have lost their minds."

"Oh, they did," Janine said, speaking of Jack's parents. "When we told them I was pregnant at nineteen, I think their first mutterings were... well, what should we do with this woman who's trapped our son?"

Maggie's lips formed a round O.

"Of course, I told them point-blank that just throwing me to the side wasn't an option since your dad and I were madly in love. And we were going to make it work with or without their approval."

"And make it work, you did," Maggie said, beaming.

"You and Alyssa and this entire party are proof of that," Janine returned as she spread her hand out toward the beautiful guests of their perfectly plotted night, the wine and cocktail drinkers, the fine suits and flawlessly manicured eyebrows and new blond highlights, just in time for summer.

At eight, everyone gathered around the tables. While Maggie and Rex sat at the head of the table, Janine and Jack sat on either side of the couple, with Janine and Alyssa to the left and right of Janine and Jack. With these great loves by her side along with a hefty dose of champagne, Janine felt all light-headed and free, as though she could have lifted off the balcony and into the clouds above.

Jack lifted his eyebrows toward her mischievously. "I guess it's time?"

Janine nodded. "You've waited for it all night."

"You're right. I have to steal the spotlight from my daughter somehow." He winked toward Maggie playfully as he rose and then clanked his fork against the side of his glass.

Slowly, the members of the party halted their conversations and turned their attention toward him. Jack held the floor, just as he always did when he wanted to. It was part of the reason Janine had fallen in love with him. She'd never met anyone like him.

"Good evening, everyone," Jack said brightly. "I'd like to welcome you to the engagement party for my eldest daughter, Magdalene Potter, better known as Maggie, one of the first great loves of my life. Horrifically for my heart, Rex has decided to steal her away from me. If you're a father of a daughter, you know how difficult this is. But you also know that when you raise a girl like Maggie, she will dive headfirst into life in a way that makes you proud. When she told me about Rex, I could hear it in her voice. She had this expectation for their future together. At the time, Rex probably thought they were just going to keep it casual. Come on, Rex. I know what men are like. And heck, my wife, Janine, knows all about that, too."

Janine chuckled, remembering how swiftly their lives had tied into one another — assuredly too quickly for Jack, who had been around twenty-two at the time and therefore had only just begun his wild party days.

"That said, just as I don't regret a single day of married life, I know neither of you will, either," Jack continued. He then lifted his glass of wine still higher and called out, "To Maggie and Rex. May you have a charmed marriage, and may your love last forever."

Across the party, everyone lifted their glasses so that they shimmered in the last light of the evening. They cheered and then sipped, which resulted in several of them beginning to turn back to their personal conversations prior to the arrival of the food.

But Janine didn't want to give all the speech-giving over to her husband. In her mind and probably in the mind of Maggie, she'd been there for much, much more throughout her life. She couldn't let Jack take all the credit. She just couldn't.

Slowly, she stood and began to tip her fork against her glass. Jack gave her a bug-eyed look, indicating that this was a misstep. Several partygoers flashed their eyes toward her. Their gazes were filled with curiosity and maybe the slightest amount of annoyance. Suddenly, Janine was reminded of her previous self — the poor girl from Brooklyn who didn't deserve a spot at the table and had married into wealth. She again turned her eyes toward Jack, who grunted, "I think we need to get on with dinner, Janny."

Janine fell back on her chair and sipped still more of her wine. He was probably right. He normally was.

Throughout dinner, Janine popped in and out of the conversations around her. If asked later, she wouldn't have been able to say what they'd discussed, as her mind was several hundred miles away. Especially as Maggie's wedding grew closer, and with Alyssa's graduation from Yale, Janine had begun to compare her relationship to her own mother and how desperately wrong everything had gone.

She had grown up with absolutely nothing. And

when Janine had been eighteen years old and ready to head off to college, (not that there had been money around for that), Nancy, her mother, had just taken off. She was gone as fast as lightning without paying rent or leaving Janine a few pennies to rub together. She'd left her completely debilitated and forced to build her life from scratch.

Goodness, how Janine wished her mother could see her just then: celebrating her daughter's wedding at one of the ritziest hotels in all of Manhattan, with her two daughters and her handsome husband at her side.

Nancy, I won. Do you hear me? And you can't hurt me anymore, she thought.

Chapter Three

The after-party at the high-rise apartment building began around eleven thirty at night. Janine felt a tiny bit bleary from wine, and she dropped into her bedroom for a moment to grip the sink of her bathroom and talk some sense into her reflection. "Just a few more hours, Janine. It's one of the best parties of your hosting career. All of Manhattan's elites look at you like you own this city."

Before she left her bedroom, she touched up her makeup and then gazed at her bed longingly. Often, Jack slept separate from her, in another bedroom, as he liked to stay up much later than she did, tending to various clients and watching sporting events. Even still, she thought she might ask him to collapse beside her that night, as she wanted him close after all the chaos of the day. Plus, he looked so deliciously handsome. She had to pinch herself sometimes to remind herself that he was still all hers after all this time.

Her husband...Her Jack.

When Janine stepped back out of the room, the party

was in full swing. She had hired a DJ — a sophisticated one that played a mixture of appropriate music, not some college-aged rapper who manned the DJ table and pumped his head in time as he adjusted the songs. A few people had gathered in the center of the room to dance with their drinks in hand. Near the kitchen, Maggie and Alyssa stood together, both holding glasses of wine. They spoke conspiratorially and then burst into giggles. Janine had long since understood that there was a great deal about her girls' relationship that she would never be allowed to know. Such was the way of sisters.

Of course, she knew she had that sort of thing with Maxine. Even though they weren't blood, they were sisters, through and through.

Speaking of, Maxine began to approach her. She slid her arm through hers and muttered, "Care to dance, honey-bunny?"

Janine laughed. "I'm so exhausted that I might topple over."

"Well, you don't look it," Maxine said as she slowly eased a curl around Janine's ear.

"Did you spot any eligible bachelors tonight?" Janine asked as she scanned the crowd.

"Unfortunately, no," Maxine returned. "Although I didn't expect much of anyone. Nobody's single these days. It's dreadful."

"Guess you'll just have to split up someone's marriage!" Janine said playfully.

"You're evil, Janine Potter. Absolutely evil."

In time, Janine and Maxine lost one another again to the ever-changing seas of the strange social circle. Janine found herself nodding along in conversation with one of Maggie's college friend's mothers, then turning around to speak with the older Italian woman Maggie had stayed with when she'd studied abroad in Milan. The woman's accent was so thick that Janine struggled to make out a single word. Instead, her smile widened, which only seemed to make the woman talk more.

At one point, she found herself again with Marcia, who leaned toward Janine, her breath laced with fiery alcohol, and whispered, "You know, I haven't told anyone."

"Told anyone what?" Janine asked, looking at her with curiosity.

"You know." Marcia waggled her eyebrows. "All that work you got done." She lifted her eyes toward Janine's eyebrows and then scanned down her face toward her breasts.

Janine laughed aloud. "What are you talking about? I haven't gotten anything done."

Marcia's lips parted. Not for the first time, Janine realized just how pudgy those lips were — as though she'd had multiple bad injections. This was so common, wasn't it? That people wanted to see themselves in everyone else, even if it wasn't true?

"You're kidding me. Are you telling me you just have fabulous genes?" Marcia demanded.

"I'm afraid she is." Maxine appeared beside her again, a fresh cocktail in hand. She beamed down at Marcia as though Janine was her prize pig at the fair. "And what's more, Janine held down her own business until about a year ago, when she took a leave of absence. She's a force of nature."

Janine's cheeks reddened. She slightly hated it when people brought up her naturopathic medicine practice, as it just reminded her that she missed it dearly. Sometimes, she struggled to remember just why she'd stepped away from it. She remembered snippets of conversations with Jack, during which he said it would have been "nice" if she'd had more time to plan some of his work functions. Had that been part of the reason? Or had she just felt stretched too thin as a Manhattan "socialite" as well as a "professional woman"? She did remember, now that she thought back, some of the snippy remarks from some of the other socialites, including Marcia, who'd said, "I can't believe your husband lets you work," as though Janine had had to clear that with him.

"Oh yes. That doctor thing you did," Marcia offered snidely.

"Doctor thing? She saved my life. Numerous times," Maxine interjected as she lifted that ever French nose of hers. "She's a saint and does amazing work, in fact. The medical world is so different without her."

Marcia seemed at a loss for words, perhaps mostly because she was drunk. She staggered back, then gripped the elbow of another woman, and cried out, "My darling, where on earth did you get that bracelet?"

Maxine and Janine made heavy eye contact. It took everything within Janine not to burst into raucous laughter.

"They're too easy, sometimes, aren't they?" Janine whispered.

"They're just paper cutouts disguised as people," Maxine returned.

Janine sipped her wine as a wave of gratefulness poured over her. "I'm just so glad you're still around, Max. Really."

Maxine shrugged. "Where the hell else would I be? Together till the end, my friend."

Janine chuckled as her eyes scanned across the crowd. "I haven't seen Jack in a while."

"I think I spotted him with some of those stuffy businessmen."

"Oh yes. That sounds about right," Janine said.

Suddenly, there was a hand across her elbow. Janine flashed her head left to find the wide, panicked eyes of her eldest daughter, Maggie. Her hand was just as cold as ice.

"Mom! I can't find my earring."

Janine sensed the alarm in her daughter's voice, and her instincts took over. No matter the problem, she was prepared to solve it, especially when it came to her daughters' happiness.

"All right. Let's retrace your steps. Don't panic."

"Mom, Rex got these for me as an engagement present..." Maggie explained as her lower lip quivered just the slightest bit. She extended a palm out to show the other, single earring, without its partner.

"Okay. Okay." Janine gave her daughter a smile. "When did you last remember having it on?"

"In the bathroom," Maggie insisted, as her words slurred together, proof of her tipsiness. "Near the foyer."

"Okay! Okay. Good place to start," Janine said. She slipped her fingers through her daughter's and guided her through the bustling crowd, toward the beautiful bathroom with the tiles they'd had shipped over from Spain the previous summer. The door was locked, so they waited until the person inside abandoned ship. Once near the sink, however, they came up dry.

"Oh, no. Rex is going to be so upset!" Maggie cried.

"I don't think that's true," Janine said. She wanted to add that if it actually was true, that if Rex got so angry with materialistic little things, then perhaps Maggie shouldn't marry him.

But of course, that was probably a topic for a different day. Not the night of the engagement party.

"Let's keep looking. Where to next?" Janine asked.

Slowly, Maggie guided her from the bathroom toward the far end of the living area, then back into the kitchen. She paused over the top of the spare appetizers, which had begun to be served to the various partygoers. "I remember it now. I had it in here. I thought maybe they were getting too heavy."

"Oh! So you probably took one of them off on purpose," Janine suggested. "That's perfect."

"Yeah! But I remember I didn't want to lose them," Maggie affirmed, her eyebrows stitching together. "So I wanted to put them somewhere safe."

"Like maybe your bedroom?"

"Sure! Maybe. That sounds right, actually," Maggie said as her eyes brightened. "Mom, I'm so sorry about this. I feel so silly."

"Honey, it happens to the best of us. You're not silly at all. It's just nerves. Now go and enjoy the rest of the evening," Janine said tenderly.

A tear rolled down Maggie's cheek, which she immediately caught. "I don't know why I'm crying. I think I'm just overwhelmed and tired," Maggie said as her shoulders shivered.

"Sure. You're allowed to be tired. Getting married is a big deal," Janine said as she collected her daughter in her arms. "Why don't you go sit down with Rex over there, and I'll head to your bedroom to find the earring? If it's not there, we can look for it after everyone is gone. I don't want to stress you out any more than you already are."

Maggie nodded somberly and then heaved a sigh. "I'm being so dramatic, Mom. I know you taught me to be better than this."

Janine watched as Rex enclosed Maggie in a warm hug. She then turned on her heel (all the while praying for a time when she could finally remove her heels) and stepped toward the back hallway, which led toward Maggie and Alyssa's old rooms. Alyssa had taken an internship for the summer, while Maggie and Rex already lived together at a loft in Brooklyn. Janine could remember when she and Jack and the girls had moved into the high-rise around fifteen years before. Maggie had been nine; Alyssa had been seven. Goodness, it had still felt like such a palace, even with the four of them. Now, it was like a ghost town, especially when Jack left on business trips.

Due to the party, the staff members had closed both Maggie's and Alyssa's bedroom doors. Without thinking, Janine stepped toward Maggie's on the left and pushed it open. She sped through the crack just as her eyes took in a view that she hadn't anticipated.

There was a couple, a man on top of a woman, on the bed.

Immediately, Janine jumped back and whipped the door partially closed so she couldn't see. She cried out at first, saying, "I'm terribly sorry!" But just as she said it, the woman of the couple cried out as well.

The scream was familiar.

It was so familiar that it made Janine's blood freeze.

It was so familiar that Janine could do nothing but grip the doorknob. It was as though time itself had taken hold of her and forced her to remain there, unable to move forward.

There was the man's voice after that.

The man's voice, as he asked, "Did you see who it was?"

"No. I didn't. My eyes were closed."

"I told you. This was too risky."

"You said nobody would come into Maggie's room. You said it would be fine."

They argued like lovers — like lovers who knew one another so well, so well that it didn't matter if you irritated the other just the tiniest bit.

"You really didn't see who it was?" the man asked.

"No. I swear. And I'm sure they didn't see, either. Everyone at this party is hammered out of their minds."

"We should get back out there. But staggered," the man said.

"I know the drill, sergeant," the woman returned. "We've been through this all before."

Janine's heart hadn't beat for a solid thirty seconds. She wondered what it would mean for her to die at her daughter's engagement party. She wondered if it would scar Maggie for life. Probably, it would.

Part of her told her to turn back.

Part of her heart screamed for her to leave the door, step back into the party, and pretend she'd never heard anything.

Everything might have been okay had she done that.

But instead, she pressed the flat of her hand against the door, and she slowly eased it open so that the creak of it was ominous, echoing from wall-to-wall of Maggie's beautiful, still pretty-pink setup.

There, standing side by side, stitching up the buttons of their various garments, were Jack and Maxine.

They looked at her.

25

They looked at her as though she was a stranger.

And she supposed, in a way, she was.

She'd entered their private space of love and romance. She felt like someone from a different universe, and she'd discovered that they had a separate language, a separate rhythm, a separate love.

She wanted to say something, but there were no words. Janine felt her head spin like she might fall at any moment. She was in complete shock. She heard the muffled words of her husband, saying, "Janine, now don't fly off the handle. It's not what it looks like."

And then there was Maxine, saying something in French which made Janine blurt out, "You haven't spoken French properly in thirty years!"

Then there was the sound of feet behind her and the appearance of their guests—several of them, whose eyes scanned from Maxine to Jack and then over to Janine, the jilted wife. It was quite simple to put together the pieces of this puzzle, to recognize what had gone wrong. In fact, in some ways, perhaps, it was the easiest thing in the world.

It was a simple formula, the way Janine's life now crumbled before her. It was as simple as one plus one. It was as easy as — French mistress? Why not also the wife's best friend?

Cliché upon cliché.

Chapter Four

Years before, when Janine and Maxine were twelve or thirteen, they had grown obsessed over their dreams at night and what their dreams might represent about their futures. Janine remembered one particular starry night when she and Maxine had stayed up till three in the morning while Janine's mother remained in the living room, smoking indoors and watching television. Nancy's moods were difficult to decipher back then, but depression largely dominated all of her emotions and actions, like a shadow.

"I saw a black dog at the edge of a driveway," Janine had said ominously on this night, and Maxine's eyes had widened. "And then, he opened his mouth, and he told me to follow him. We walked through the woods toward a large cave with an opening like a mouth, and from the edge of the cave, as I peered in, I could see the entire island of Manhattan. It was just there, inside the cave. The dog asked me if I wanted to jump into the cave, but I knew that if I did, I would fall to my death on 44th Street."

At this, Maxine had laughed uproariously. "Shh!" Janine's eyes had flashed. "Don't let Mom know we're still awake."

"I don't think she cares," Maxine had pointed out. "She's probably just glad to have some company at this hour."

Janine's stomach had tightened at the thought. She knew very well that her mother was lonely. At thirteen, she supposed this was the sort of thing you began to pick up on in adults. But it wasn't as though she was equipped to understand how to help her mother. In many ways, her depression and loneliness made her angry, as she felt them like blockades between her and Nancy and this other fantastical life of luxury. (Although, of course, the concept of luxury was a faraway one in Brooklyn.)

"What do you think my dream means?" Janine had finally asked.

Maxine had fluttered her fingers in the air between them as though this would conjure the spirit of Freud himself to come explain it. "I think it means that one day, a long time from now, you will be very rich."

"Wow. Rich, huh?"

"Yes. But it will come at a great cost to your soul," Maxine had added, just before erupting in uncontrollable laughter — enough to make Nancy bound into the room and demand that the two of them quiet down, if only so she could hear her television show.

* * *

It had been two weeks since Maggie's engagement party.

Janine sat upright in an enormous California king bed, located in the center of a grand suite in the Lotte

New York Palace. She was dressed in a plush robe, no makeup, and sunlight from a glorious day in late May streamed through the curtains and cast its glow across the bed. She had been at the Lotte since everything had exploded, and she'd hardly seen another living soul in all that time. She hadn't even informed her daughters of her precise location, as she didn't want them storming in and catching sight of her like this. If anything, she kept them at bay with phone calls.

Like this— at the end of her rope and in the middle of a nervous breakdown, questioning every single thing that had ever happened to her — from her love of Jack to every conversation she'd ever had with Maxine, trying to figure out what went wrong and when it went wrong. Why hadn't she seen it coming? Were there any signs, and if there were, why had she missed them?

Janine had always thought the idea of imagining your own downfall was a bit perverse. She'd never been particularly fascinated with "true crime," like several New York socialites she'd previously run around with, as she hadn't liked imagining that those sorts of horrible things could actually happen. She also hadn't been so into stories about natural disasters or even reading about whatever horrors the news had to offer. *"Why should I darken my thoughts with reality when there is so much good in the world for me to appreciate?"* she'd said once to Maxine.

Maxine had, in turn, told her that she lived in a fantasy world.

Janine supposed that was true. Especially now.

Although she willed herself not to, Janine picked up her phone and flicked toward the stories on the local blogosphere, the various social media-famous New York socialites, along with the gossip columnists who normally wrote such stellar things about Janine and her family and the money they had and the parties they threw.

Naturally, the conversation surrounding Janine had altered a great deal over the previous weeks.

The first one had come out the day after Janine had moved into the Lotte New York Palace. The headline had burned holes into the back of her skull:

Manhattan Socialite Maxine Aubert Steals Jack Potter from Best Friend

One thing that had particularly stung about that headline was that Janine's name hadn't even been included. Maxine and Jack, Jack and Maxine — the world buzzed for them, despite not knowing them at all. Of course, when headlines and various publications began to list Janine's name, she hated that just as much, and perhaps even more.

"Janine Potter thought she had it all. She married the son of an oil tycoon, Jack Potter, had his two daughters, and went on to be just another Manhattan socialite, a woman who lives out her days some forty floors above the rest of us, whose only cares involve which tiles she might want to order in from say, Italy, to switch up the décor of one of her five bathrooms. But all that changed on the night of her daughter's engagement party when she, along with several of this writer's sources, discovered her husband in the throes of passion with her very best friend, Maxine Aubert.

"The events that transpired after this initial discovery are difficult to decipher. It's clear to this writer that many of the high-rollers at this particular affair (poor choice of word, perhaps) had more than a few drinks. However, apparently, Janine reached for a vase on the nearest book-shelf and flung the thing at their heads, only for it to shatter somewhere behind them. She then screamed for everyone to get the hell out of her penthouse!"

Janine furrowed her brow at the words. It was as though she read a story of someone else's life, someone else's collapse. She had no memory of saying any of that nor of throwing a vase at their heads. Perhaps these things had happened, but there was no way to know, although they certainly didn't sound like things the Janine Potter she'd always known would do.

That said, the Janine Potter she'd always known had basically left the building. In her place, she'd left this creature, in a plush robe, who hadn't left her hotel room in four days' time.

Depression. Anxiety. Fear. Mortification. There were a number of words for her current state. It was difficult for Janine to imagine herself digging her way out of whatever this was.

The only person on the planet who knew where she was (beyond the hotel staff, who probably gossiped) was Jack Potter himself. After all, he owned the credit card she had used to check herself in. For this reason, he'd already sent her a note, which she had read exactly once two nights prior before she'd vomited up the contents of her stomach and spent the next fourteen hours horizontal.

"We will divorce. Don't dwell on the possibility of a reunion."

There had been more to the letter but not much. Janine knew better than to argue with Jack. He no longer loved her. He saw no reason to continue their marriage after such a scandal, to pretend he still loved her, so he'd decided to throw in the towel once and for all and toss her out like a piece of trash.

31

But then, what was Maxine to him? Janine wasn't sure she wanted to know or if she had the strength to know.

Oh, but she was more beautiful. And funnier. And trendier. As her best friend, Janine had been proud of these features of Maxine. Now, they'd flipped themselves over, and she stirred with the kind of jealousy that could eat you from the inside.

Suddenly, there was a knock on the door. Janine's heart pounded in her chest so hard she thought it might rupture. She hadn't ordered room service. She gripped the edge of her robe as anxiety spun through her. She was terrified that somehow, the gossip columnists or the paparazzi had caught wind of her location. She imagined opening the door to find flashing cameras, all of which would catch her looking haphazard in her robe, hair undone, and wearing no makeup.

When the knock rang out again, there was a voice that accompanied it. It was sweet and light, and it triggered something in Janine's mind. The third knock brought the voice a bit louder. It sounded like it said, "Mom?"

Finally, Janine trudged across the suite. Frightened, she pressed her hand against the door and said, "Maggie? Is that you?"

The voice on the other side was muffled but relieved. "Mom! Yes. It's us—Alyssa and me. Dad told us where to find you. Open up, okay? Please."

Janine yanked open the door to find her beautiful daughters standing before her. They wore springtime dresses, which shimmered lightly toward the tops of their thighs, and their dark curls wafted beautifully across their shoulders. Their eyebrows were furrowed, and Alyssa looked as though she'd spent the past hour or so crying.

Without another word, Alyssa flung herself toward her mother and let out a gut-wrenching sob. Janine's motherly instincts took over, so much so that she nearly forgot her own trauma. She stepped back and held Alyssa tightly as Maggie entered the hotel suite and pushed the door closed.

When the hug broke, Janine glanced up to view Maggie's expression — one of shock and fear. Her eyes scanned the hotel suite, which wasn't really dirty or anything, but of course, there were empty bottles of wine on the table and several boxes from take-out food. Janine hadn't allowed the maids inside the room for a few days, and probably, the place had a musty scent she just didn't notice. Probably, the musty scent came from her own body.

"Mom. You can't live here like this," Maggie whispered. Her face was marred with concern and fear.

With a jolt, Janine was reminded of herself with her own mother, Nancy — all the judgment she'd cast on the woman, who hadn't been able to give her a life of prosperity and comfort. She'd had trouble with alcohol. She had dated all the wrong men. Janine wanted to insist that she was nothing like her mother, especially now, although since Maggie and Alyssa hardly knew their grandmother, she knew this would sound like jibberish to them. Probably, they would want to her to undergo an assessment, put her under observation until she started to make sense. (There had been talk of doing this with Nancy when Janine had been around eleven, and Janine had been terrified of the concept ever since.)

Of course, The Lotte Hotel was a far cry from the world Janine and Nancy had fumbled around in back in the '80s and '90s. This wasn't the time to point that out, though. Not with Maggie and Alyssa looking the way they did.

"Mom, you know it's only three in the afternoon, right?" Alyssa asked as she pointed at the half-drunk glass of wine on the bedside table.

Janine didn't say anything. If she was honest, she would tell them it was her third of the day. This made her stomach swirl with shame. This was her mother's game, not hers.

Maggie grabbed her mother's hands, looked at her with tears in her eyes, and said, "Mom, I love you so much. We love you so much, and it kills us to see you hurting like this. What Dad did...What Maxine did. It's inexcusable, and we're completely disgusted with them both."

Alyssa took a step closer to both of them and grabbed her mother's hand as well. "Everything Maggie is saying is true. We're so disgusted and angry with Dad right now that we're not even talking to him."

"Mom, I know this is hard, but you have to rise above. Hold your head high even though you're hurting. We're here for you," Maggie finished as a tear rolled down her cheek.

Janine wiped it away from her cheek with the pad of her thumb and felt her own tears fall. She let out a little gasp before saying, "You girls are too smart for your own good. You know that?"

Both girls laughed through their tears and Janine followed suit as they talked a little more. After a half-hour had passed, Maggie looked over at Alyssa before saying, "I think we should get out of here."

Janine arched an eyebrow. "I'm not going anywhere."

"Mom. When was the last time you, I don't know, ate

a salad?" Alyssa demanded as she pointed at various pizza boxes.

"We could just go into the Village for some nutrients. Maybe a green smoothie?" Maggie coaxed.

"Girls, I really shouldn't leave the hotel," Janine returned. She crossed her arms over her chest as a wave of fear crashed over her.

"Mom, we haven't seen you in two weeks..." Alyssa said softly. "You didn't tell us where you were! We had to find out from Dad."

"We've been talking on the phone. You both knew I was fine," Janine returned.

"Yeah. But we've just been out there. Dealing with all of this on our own," Maggie pointed out.

"You're not the only one whose life fell apart that night," Alyssa said somberly.

Janine had to hand it to them. When they wanted it, they could be manipulative. Maybe this was Jack's personality, shining through her beautiful daughters. They had a point, though.

Even still, if she dressed carefully and hid enough, perhaps nobody would notice her. She dropped her chin to her chest and heaved a sigh.

"You really can't hide for the rest of your life, Mom," Alyssa whispered as she placed a hand on her mother's shoulder.

"This isn't a Dickens novel," Maggie affirmed. "People move on with their lives after stuff like this. You're young and so, so, smart, Mom."

"You can get through this," Alyssa insisted. "We've got you."

Janine looked at both her girls with defeat and turned toward the bathroom. Just before she headed to the shower, she gripped her wineglass and took a sip. If she was going to make an attempt to head back out into the world, into the springtime that surrounded Manhattan, then she wanted a drink to help her along.

She was beginning to understand her mother, Nancy, more and more as the days passed. How dreadful.

Chapter Five

Daphne's Green Garden was a millennial-friendly hangout in Greenwich Village and one of Alyssa and Maggie's favorite spots. Janine had been there a handful of times with them, the last time, most notably about a month before, when they'd gone over the details of the engagement party and fantasized about how marvelous it would be. Hindsight, as usual, was twenty-twenty.

Janine had donned a pair of sunglasses and a vintage scarf, which she'd purchased at one of the market stalls in Paris on her recent trip with Maxine. When she glanced at her reflection in the mirror at the restaurant, she saw an old woman from an Alfred Hitchcock movie peering back at her.

They ordered. Janine heard herself say something about a "garden omelet," although, as she handed the menu back to the server, she had little recollection of what that actually was. Alyssa and Maggie eyed her as though she was on the verge of a meltdown. Janine thought about asking them if she'd actually thrown a vase at Jack's head but then thought better of it. Forward motion was key.

"So. Maggie. How is Rex?"

Maggie gave a slight shrug. "He's fine. We're all fine."

"Alyssa? Your internship?"

"It's good, Mom. I have the week off," Alyssa said.

"Oh. Why is that?"

"It's Memorial Day, Mom." Alyssa explained it as though Janine was a bit slow in the head or a child.

"Is it? That happened fast." Janine's eyes flicked toward the alcohol menu, which remained on the table between them. Perhaps she should have gone for a mimosa.

Alyssa splayed her hand across her mother's. The silence stretched between them. Maggie and Alyssa seemed to urge each other to be the next to speak. Maybe they'd rehearsed some kind of pep talk.

"Your father wrote me. We will be moving forward with the divorce." Janine tried out the words just to see how they felt. They felt awful. They scraped against her tongue like hot knives.

Alyssa's shoulders quaked. She looked on the verge of tears again. "Oh, Mom. No."

"Someone mentioned that you maybe—" Maggie furrowed her brow as she struggled to speak.

"That I did what?"

"That maybe you signed a prenup?" Alyssa blurted.

Janine's eyes widened. A laugh ballooned from her stomach and erupted from her lips. She'd hardly even considered that!

"Well. Of course, I did," she said. Her voice remained light. "I was madly in love with Jack Potter. I thought he would never leave me. His family demanded a prenup be signed. I had no choice in the matter. It doesn't matter."

Again, silence fell. Alyssa and Maggie seemed to have a quiet conversation over the table while Janine returned her attention to the alcohol menu. *Maybe a Bloody Mary was a better order? Or straight to wine again.*

At that moment, a woman appeared over their table. Janine blinked up into the familiar eyes of Kennedy Hollingsworth, one of the Manhattan socialites who'd, of course, been at the engagement party. The women gazed down at Janine as though Janine was a prized cow. Janine's heart actually dropped into the basement of her belly.

"Janine Potter! My, my. I didn't imagine I'd see the likes of you around the Village."

Had Janine ever liked Kennedy Hollingsworth? She couldn't remember having a single conversation with the woman who had ever filled her with anything beyond disdain, hatred, and boredom.

"Kennedy. Hello."

"And the girls!" Kennedy said brightly. "Alyssa and Maggie. Always such beauties."

Alyssa and Maggie muttered thanks as their eyes turned toward Janine in utter panic. This was precisely why Janine hadn't wanted to leave the hotel; even her disguise hadn't worked.

"Janine, I am glad I caught you." Kennedy's eyes glittered with malice, even as her words seemed to attempt to "comfort." "I just can't believe what Maxine put you through. Sure, husbands cheat. But dear friends, like Maxine was to you? I just don't know how anyone could handle that. Really. If you ever need someone to chat with—"

Oh, but Kennedy had done enough. The words sliced through Janine, body and soul, and she erupted with sorrow. Tears rolled down her cheeks, dragging along the dark makeup from her eyes, and she poured herself over the table. Her surroundings no longer mattered. Kennedy no longer mattered. All she could think was — yeah — exactly right, Kennedy. Maxine had been her greatest love. She'd thought of her above Jack in many ways.

And now, she had nothing—no Maxine. No husband.

She was pathetic.

"I think my mother has been through enough, thank you. Now, if you'll excuse us," Maggie blurted angrily to the rude woman.

Somehow, Maggie and Alyssa gathered Janine up and led her out into the drenching sunlight. Maggie hailed a cab as Alyssa muttered words of comfort. All the while, Janine dropped further into a daze.

Janine awoke several hours later. She was on her back in what seemed to be Maggie's apartment's guest room. She recognized the wallpaper, which she and Maggie had agonized over the previous summer (the choice of it, not the installation, as they'd naturally hired someone else to do that). She wondered why the girls hadn't taken her back to the hotel.

Then she thought, with a jolt, that perhaps because she and Jack were getting divorced, and she'd signed that stupid prenup — perhaps Jack had asked the girls to get her out of the hotel so he could stop paying for it.

Were Alyssa and Maggie in on all of this?

Disgruntled, Janine reached for her phone on the bedside table. After only a few now-familiar clicks, she made her way to several gossip columns. One of them had already featured her apparent "meltdown" in the Village.

Janine splayed her hand over her forehead in shock. She had known better than to leave the hotel. Her emotional state was on its last straw, at best.

There was a knock on the door. Before Janine had a chance to answer, Maggie opened it. She wore an apron, and her hair was in an updo, and she peered in at Janine as though she were the mother, and Janine, the daughter.

"Hi." Janine wasn't sure what else to say. She flicked her phone to the side so as not to be caught looking over such trash.

"Hi." Maggie didn't sound pleased. "You passed out in the cab."

Janine heaved a sigh. "That must have been really scary, Maggie. I'm so sorry."

"Scary, yes. But mostly, I'm terrified that you aren't taking care of yourself," Maggie said slowly. She stepped into the shadowed room and pushed the door closed.

Janine felt like an animal at the zoo.

"You're going to run into people like Kennedy all the time, Mom," Maggie continued. "You have to find a way to deal with this. I know it's not fair, but you have to."

Janine was reminded of a long-ago afternoon when Maggie had arrived home crying after a boy she'd liked had told her he didn't like her back. Janine and Maxine had comforted Maggie in every way they'd known how— in ways they'd previously comforted one another when teenage boys had done them wrong. They'd eaten Oreos with peanut butter, and they'd watched rom-coms. Janine imagined Maxine coming in after Maggie and saying, "All right. Enough of this. Let's get you out of bed."

But of course, Maxine would do no such thing. She hadn't even bothered to call.

Not that there was anything to say.

Maggie grumbled, then lifted her phone from her pocket. Behind her, the door rattled with another knock as her fiancé, Rex, called out, "Mags? I'm gonna head down to the Ritters for that barbecue. You still want to come?"

Maggie's eyes were difficult to read. She shifted her weight as Janine muttered, "Maggie, please. Don't stay home on my account. Besides, I should really get back to the hotel."

Rex remained outside the door. After a pause, Maggie hollered, "I don't think so, Rex."

"Maybe just for a beer or something?"

Maggie sounded doubtful. "Maybe."

The newly engaged couple said their love you's as Janine dropped her chin toward her chest with shame. There was a heaviness to her current sadness, something that told her it would be very, very difficult to walk herself even from this bed to the bathroom in the hall.

"I just got a message from someone," Maggie said suddenly.

"Oh?" Janine struggled to sound interested.

"It's um. Well. I don't know how to tell you, so I'm just going to say it," Maggie continued. She looked on the verge of tears. "It was Grandma Nancy."

Janine's eyes flashed toward Maggie's. She felt her facial features harden. Sure, Maggie was twenty-four now and could certainly handle herself. Still, Janine hadn't spoken with Nancy in over a decade, and she knew very little about her current life — only that at some point, she'd married someone. She had no way to know if that marriage had lasted or how her mother was, physically or mentally. Knowing what she knew about Nancy, Janine didn't want to think about her mother's current mental status.

"Say something, Mom," Maggie breathed.

"You know how I feel about Grandma," Janine returned.

"You two have a lot of bad blood between you. I know that." Maggie swung a dark strand around her ear. "But you mentioned a few years ago that maybe Grandma had changed since she married someone? And she wasn't very old when everything happened between the two of you. She had you, at what? Age sixteen?"

"I ran out of sympathy for Nancy a long, long time ago," Janine said somberly.

"Don't you at least want to know what the message said?"

Janine crossed and uncrossed her hands on her thighs. "Probably something about the divorce, I guess. The very public, very famous divorce. And about Maxine. She used to call Maxine one of her daughters."

Maggie sucked in her cheeks. "She knows about it, yeah. But she also said, well, that if you want to get out of the city sometime, she has a place for you to stay. She knows how much you love the city. But she also thinks it's poison and this could do you some good. I think she might be right."

"Poison, huh?" Janine held her daughter's eyes, even as she wanted to roll her own all the way back into her skull. "She really has a flair for the dramatic, doesn't she?"

Almost immediately, Janine regretted her words. After all, wasn't she the one who'd holed up in a hotel for two weeks, avoiding her daughters, hiding from the world? Hadn't she been the one to have a breakdown at a Greenwich Village brunch spot? And now, wasn't she back in bed?

"Right." Maggie looked at a complete loss. "Well.

43

Anyway. I just wanted to let you know because we don't keep things from each other."

Janine dropped her eyes to her hands. This was a call-out, proof that her daughters were angry that she'd hidden herself away for so long.

"Let me know if you need anything," Maggie said softly. "I'll just be in the living room."

"You should go to that barbecue, Mags."

"No. I don't feel up to it," Maggie returned. She then bit her lower lip and added, "I'm so angry with Dad, Mom. I don't know how I'll ever be able to look at him the same—let alone Maxine."

Janine's lower lip quivered as she pulled her daughter in for a much-needed embrace. They stayed like that for a moment until they collected themselves. She resented Jack all the more for what he'd done to their daughters. They had always pledged that the girls came first in everything. Yes, they were twenty-four and twenty-two and old enough to handle it; still, as Janine knew, you never really got over the fact that your family was a busted-up mess.

When Maggie left the bedroom, Janine tidied herself as best as she could in the mirror, gathered her things, and appeared in the foyer a little while later. Maggie blinked up from her book, her face marred with confusion.

"Where are you going?"

"I don't want to be a burden on you, Maggie. I never want that."

Maggie dropped her book to the side and rushed to her feet. "You're not, Mom."

"Well, I feel like I am. I'll see you soon, honey. Just — please. Remember. You didn't do anything wrong in this. It's nobody's fault. It's just what life is."

Chapter Six

The following morning, the hotel concierge rang Janine's suite to inform her that the credit card she'd given them had recently been declined. Janine, who was privy to the multiple, multiple zeroes in Jack Potter's expansive piggy bank, expressed shock at this news.

"There must be some kind of mistake," she told him. "That card is nowhere close to being expired."

"I'm afraid it no longer works, madam. We will need you to arrange another payment option with us. As soon as you can," the man returned promptly. There was no haughtiness to his words, for, in his mind, he thought the likes of Janine Potter could arrange for another payment with the wave of her hand.

Janine took an overly long shower. In there, she screamed into her palms and felt the scalding water tear through her skin. She felt like she was losing every ounce of sanity she had left in her.

For the first time since Maggie had mentioned it, her mother's offer hovered in the back of Janine's mind. It felt

45

like a safety raft, something to cling to until the waves calmed down. Still, after all the trauma and horror that she and her mother had been through, Janine felt it was against her mental and physical well-being to return to her. Their lives together had been borderline hell. When Nancy left the city, Janine had pledged to never, ever wind up like Nancy. And she hadn't.

At least, she thought she'd avoided it. Yet here she was. Screaming in a shower, just as her mother had sometimes, when the money had run dry all over again, and there was nothing to do but hover in the still-hot water, as it kept the mind off things like hunger.

When Janine had first met Jack, and he'd begun to spoil her with so many things, including taking her out to the fanciest restaurants, she'd started to put on weight in a way that pleased her. She'd loved her round hips and her supple thighs; she'd loved the soft curve of her cheeks. Rather soon after that, her belly extended too far out, and she'd learned she was pregnant with Maggie. An accident. A beautiful accident— one that had changed her entire life.

Janine crammed various items into her suitcase. Throughout the past two weeks, she had hardly worn a thing she'd brought from home, and now, she acknowledged just how silly some of the items were. A dress she'd purchased in Rome to go out to dinner with her husband. A pair of stilettos, just in case she wanted to party alone in her room and tower over absolutely nobody. Then the makeup and perfume she'd brought — which she had barely used at all.

It wasn't completely necessary that she depart. Due to her naturopathic medicine practice, she had some funds in the bank – enough to linger on at the hotel a little while longer. Still, it felt pathetic. And in truth, if she was about to build a life of her own, she needed those funds. The likes of the Lotte weren't exactly kosher for her any longer.

When Janine appeared on the sidewalk in front of the hotel, she blinked out at the now June late-morning, a marvelous day in a city she loved, a city that, in almost every way, reflected her body and soul. She'd seen the worst and the very best of it.

And now, she felt she had nowhere to turn. The city had somehow rejected her. She was a crumpled, used-up wife of a very wealthy man and a mother whose children no longer needed her or so she thought. And, as ever, a girl who felt she didn't have a mother to call her own.

Janine still had cash to pay for a taxi to make her way back to her apartment. A funny itch in the back of her mind thought it would be a funny thing to just march in and return to her life as though nothing had happened. She imagined Jack coming in from work, removing his suit jacket, and asking her how her day had gone. They would sidestep the issue. No, Maxine would never return to their lives, but that was all right. Maxine could go to Paris for all Janine cared. She could take over Europe if only she'd leave New York in Janine's capable hands.

The doorman did, in fact, ogle Janine as she entered, so much so that she actually gave him a cutting look and said, "Take a picture. Everyone else seems to want to." She then ducked onto the elevator and pushed a button to rocket herself into the sky.

Her apartment was spick and span and utterly empty. It looked like nobody had been inside its walls for several days, which wasn't a crazy thought, as Jack did travel for business quite a lot (at least, she'd thought that — but maybe he was just headed to Maxine's every time?).

She walked the familiar path toward her bedroom. The bed was made, and sunlight streamed in beautifully through the windows. Fresh flowers had been cut and placed in a vase near the window, which was something Janine had requested the maids do daily. She remembered having that request, yes, but also felt it was one of the strangest things she'd ever done. How could she go from those awful childhood days where they scrambled just to put food on the table to demanding fresh flowers every day?

Perspective was a strange thing. She felt she had gotten more than enough of it the previous few weeks.

Janine sat on the edge of her bed for a long time and pondered what to do. She could check herself into another hotel? Something cheaper? Somewhere she could draw the curtains and just sleep?

As if on cue, she received a text message from Jack.

> JACK: When you get over your nervous breakdown, we need to discuss logistics.

Wow! So he'd canceled the card as a way to bring her close to him again if only so he could nail down the final details of their separation and divorce. He had more money than God — a statement he'd made once, in fact, which meant that it was no skin off his back to help Janine out with a hotel.

He just wanted her good and gone and not lurking somewhere in the distance, latched to his credit card. He didn't want to "deal" with her.

Janine stood from the edge of the bed and walked like

a zombie toward her bathroom. Once in there, she splashed cold water on her cheeks and blinked at her reflection. She looked tired, worn, and her cheeks were hollowed out. Back in the old days, she and Maxine had practiced sucking their cheeks in as a way to keep up with some of the high-rolling, beautiful wives of the rich men who were friends with their husbands. Maxine and Janine had always known that every night out with them was a night of competition — who had the best wife? Who had the best life?

As she tapped a cloth over her cheeks to dry, her eyes dropped toward a pair of earrings on the marble counter. Her heart thudded with sudden panic. She thought maybe that she would collapse on the tiles.

These earrings belonged to Maxine. Janine knew because she'd been there when Maxine had purchased them the previous summer at a little place in Tribeca. Janine backed away from the earrings as though they were explosives. She then stepped into the hallway and scurried for the kitchen, where she found still more signs of her dearly beloved best friend in the world. There sat Maxine's familiar hand cream, which she had shipped in from Paris. Beside it sat a little purse.

Slowly, Janine stepped out toward the living room, where she realized that one of the bedroom doors had been closed the entire time. This was the door to the room in which Jack slept frequently.

She supposed it was some kind of service to her, not being together in her bedroom, which her sacred space.

If Jack and Maxine actually were home, then they hadn't budged from bed in the previous fifteen minutes since Janine's arrival. Janine stared at the closed door and willed it to remain closed. She couldn't face them. Seeing the earrings and the purse and the hand cream had already been enough.

This was her home. It had been her home. For so many, many years, she'd felt safe there.

Now, she felt she might fall through the floorboards or have a heart attack in the very center of the living room. Jack and Maxine would find her on that rug they'd purchased from Morocco. The one Jack had said would "bring the room together."

There wasn't time to waste. Janine felt poisoned — by the city, by her life, by her husband, by each and every decision that had led her to this point. She had to get away.

But she couldn't go to Boston and run to Alyssa's little apartment.

And she really couldn't manage facing Maggie again, not with the way she looked at her, with so much despair. Her eyes were so hollow, so fearful that her mother was about to go off the rails.

How was it that Janine had only one answer? How was it that this was her conclusion?

In five minutes' time, Janine packed as much as she could into two suitcases. She grabbed one of her favorite photo albums, which included photos of her and her daughters from fifteen years before when they'd visited Maine together without Jack. When she flicked through, another photo fell out, as it didn't belong to the collection. There, at her feet, was a photo of herself and Maxine. They looked to be in their mid-twenties, ready to take on the world. Maxine held Maggie in her arms as Maggie laughed and had her fingers in her mouth.

The photo mocked her.

She stepped toward her bathroom and placed the photograph beneath Maxine's earrings for her to find later. She wanted Maxine to know that she would never forget this. She wanted Maxine to know that this ultimate betrayal had ruined both of their lives, in a way.

Yet still, she couldn't believe it.

Janine left her keys on the counter, collected her things, and headed for the elevator. Her mind screamed as she stepped out; her body ached for her to return to that previous comfort. But in truth, there was nothing for her there any longer.

Jack didn't have to hold her hostage for her to cooperate.

And no — maybe she wouldn't get much of his money in the divorce.

But she'd been through worse, hadn't she? She'd always come out on top. It was the Janine Grimson way, pre-Potter.

When she found her car in the garage, she placed the suitcases in the back trunk tenderly, realizing that she hadn't been the one to put her own suitcases in a car in probably twenty years. She found she liked performing such a task. It reminded her that with this lack of privilege and fortune, she would be able to free herself of this world she no longer belonged to.

Maybe that was something to celebrate. That, and the full tank of gas, that would surely get her all the way to Woods Hole, Massachusetts, where the ferry left for Martha's Vineyard, where her mother resided.

Chapter Seven

Janine arrived in Falmouth about an hour after the last ferry departed. As she was limited on funds, she checked herself into a middle-of-the-road hotel and paid in cash, which she watched the front desk manager count out in front of her, his lips moving as he whispered the count-up to himself. When his eyes flashed up to her, he feasted on her: her expensive earrings, her beautiful makeup, her clothing, straight from Paris. She looked every bit like a Manhattan socialite, yet she was stationed there, at the hotel just south of the highway exit. She was a fish out of water.

The front desk manager hesitated as though he wanted to drum up the courage to ask her why she was there. But hotels were havens of secrecy, and he evenly slid into his actual question, which was, "Are you headed to the Vineyard?"

Janine nodded. "I am."

"I assume you've been there before?"

"Never," Janine told him.

His eyes widened just the slightest bit as he leaned

forward. "It's one of the most magical places in the world."

The words rattled around in Janine's skull as she investigated her little, shadowed hotel room. From the window, she could see the highway, where headlights skidded across the top-line and guided the little cars' routes home. The room had a small television, a rug the color of blood, and a bathroom with tiny, generic soaps. The room had a strange smell, one that had no relation at all to the lavender scents that had flourished through her hotel room in Manhattan.

"Look at your life, Janine Grimson," she breathed. *"This is where you belong."*

When Janine couldn't sleep, she noticed her daughter was on the messaging service they both used. After a pause, Janine called her. Maggie answered almost immediately.

"Hi, Maggie." Janine swallowed the lump in her throat. "I wanted to let you know that I got to Falmouth."

"Was the drive okay?" Maggie asked softly. "I can't remember the last time I saw you drive."

"It was just like riding a bike," Janine told her, although this wasn't technically true. She'd spent a lot of the drive with her hands gripping the steering wheel way too tightly, as other vehicles had whizzed around her and occasionally blared their horns.

"That's good to hear."

Behind Maggie's voice, Janine heard the sound of the TV. Janine could imagine the view: Maggie and Rex, all cuddled up after a long day, watching one of their favorite prestige drama TV shows.

"What did Grandma Nancy say when you called her?" Maggie asked.

"Not a lot. She just said she has a room for me at her place. And that her husband died this year."

"That's so sad," Maggie murmured.

"It is." In truth, Janine wasn't sure what she felt about it. She'd never known this man. Maybe he'd saved her mother's life. Maybe he had been her true love. Maybe she would never really know why he'd mattered.

"But she just feels like a stranger," Janine added, which was maybe a step too far. "I hadn't heard her voice in over ten years."

"I told you. You can come back up to the city and stay with us if you want to," Maggie said. "If this is too much for you."

Janine couldn't express just how pathetic it felt to lean on her children like this. "It's okay. I already drove all the way here. I might as well spend the time to figure things out and see what my mother has been up to all these years."

"Maybe she'll surprise you," Maggie offered.

"Maybe." Janine's voice was doubtful. Her mother had, in fact, surprised her a number of times over the years: when she had tried to get sober and failed; when she'd forgotten to pick Janine up from daycare, and they hadn't been able to track her down until nightfall; when she had forgotten to do laundry for so many days that their house had begun to reek, which had led Janine to do her first load of laundry around age five.

"A lot of time has passed. Things change," Maggie reminded her.

"Oh yes. That's one thing I know better than most. Things do, indeed, change," Janine repeated her daughter's words. Just before she hung up, the silence was deafening when she finally said, "Honey, I love you."

"I love you too, Mom."

Janine tossed and turned most of the night. Each time she opened her eyes, she found herself struggling to remember where she was. Once, around two in the morning, she reached a hand out in the bed as though she was searching for Jack. All she got was the emptiness that was beside her and the feel of the hotel comforter, which had probably been used by thousands and thousands of strangers. She had never felt quite this alone before.

The following morning, Janine drove toward Woods Hole, where the ferry departed. She parked her car in long-term parking and walked over to the ferry docks, where she purchased a one-way ticket from a teenager with a visor on the top of his head. He pointed toward the ramp, which led up to the boat, and she thanked him while another ferry worker hustled up to take her suitcases and pile them on a luggage cart. She was grateful not to have to lug them with her onto the ferry.

The little cafe on board sold what looked like stale muffins and thick black coffee that had sat too long. She bought both as her stomach threatened to eat itself, and she nibbled at the edge of the muffin while she gazed out at the ocean beyond the window. The water churned brightly beneath the enormous June sky. It seemed unlikely that a cloud would form to threaten such a beautiful summer day.

Janine thought something was menacing about such nice weather, especially on this day when her life was in shambles— that she would return to her mother like a wounded animal. Rain would have been more fitting: that and hailstones.

The ferry arrived in Oak Bluffs at ten in the morning. She joined the bustling vacationers as they marched onto the docks and collected their luggage. As she waited, Janine scanned her surroundings. The island seemed like an oasis, far from the madness of New York City, and she couldn't help but think it was somehow too perfect, with the sailboats that dotted the surrounding docks, and the old-world buildings, and the gorgeous, sun-tanned people who looked absolutely smitten with one another and the island itself.

When Janine grabbed her suitcases, she turned toward the main road, where she hunted for the Katama Lodge and Wellness Spa vehicle, which her mother had arranged to pick her up. Sure enough, there was a tan-colored van with the business logo written across it, hovering just to the right of the docks. She marched up to the passenger window and rapped the glass gently. The driver leaped up with surprise, then delivered her a welcoming smile.

The driver appeared on the sidewalk a second later. He was broad-shouldered, with a pot-belly, approximately sixty years old, with hazel eyes and gray-blond hair.

"You must be Janine!" he said as he beamed at her. "And goodness, I guess you get this all the time, but you look so much like your mother. Both beauties!"

Janine had resented this back in her teenage years. No matter how terrible her mother had treated herself back then, her genes had sustained her. Plus, she was only sixteen years older than Janine herself, which meant that now — at forty-three and fifty-nine, they were comparable in age. Right there in the middle of life.

"Hi," Janine tried as her throat constricted. "You work for my mother?"

"I worked for the Katama Lodge and Wellness Spa,"

the man explained as he stepped around to open the trunk. "But it hasn't reopened since Neal's passing; God rest his soul."

The man placed both suitcases in the back and then smacked his palms together. "I still help Nancy out when she needs me. I've been a friend of the Remington family for decades. I can't imagine not stepping in whenever possible."

The Remington family. The one her mother had married into.

The man snapped the trunk closed and then opened the back door for Janine to enter. "My name is Jeff," he explained. "Jeff Maxfield."

"Nice to meet you," Janine said as she eased inside the vehicle.

They fell into silence as Jeff drove through Oak Bluffs. Janine's eyes ate up everything — the quaint architecture, the beautiful houses, the people, as they walked hand in hand down the sidewalk.

"I'm sorry to hear the Katama Lodge closed," Janine tried then.

Jeff cleared his throat. "It was horrible when Neal died. Nancy and the girls weren't sure what to do. Especially Elsa. She loved that father of hers to pieces. And gosh, she's been through a lot herself over the years. Nancy said it was best for everyone to take a step back and regroup."

"Do you think it'll reopen?"

"I don't know," Jeff said. "I certainly hope so. It was one of the better gigs I ever had. I'm working now as a driver for a hotel in Edgartown, and it's just not the same."

Janine marveled at the way Jeff spoke of her mother.

It felt as though Nancy was a distant person she'd never met, unconnected to the events of their shared past.

They drove for several minutes and turned out of Oak Bluffs. Janine spotted a golf course on her left, where Martha's Vineyard's elite golfers stood out beneath the eggshell blue sky and whipped balls across the green.

"I'd love to be out there today!" Jeff said while he gripped the steering wheel.

"Yeah," Janine agreed, although she'd never played golf in her life.

When they turned down another road, there was a sudden thump, and the entire car yanked to the right, onto the shoulder of the road. Janine's heart thudded as Jeff said, "Whoa! What was that?" He stopped the vehicle and yanked his head around. "I think we hit something!"

"Oh, no." Janine splayed her hand across her forehead. This felt like a bad omen.

Jeff checked to make sure nobody drove up behind them, then stepped outside and rushed to the right-hand side of the car. There, he bent down to inspect the tire. Janine opened her door, careful not to look down, just in case.

"A-ha!" he said.

"What happened?"

"There's a nail in the tire!" he replied.

"Shoot."

"Not to worry. I have a spare in the back," he said. He snapped back upright and headed toward the trunk while Janine closed the door again and leaned back against the leather seat.

In a way, this actually felt like a blessing now. It pushed back the time when she'd meet her mother again. It delayed the inevitable.

Time passed. Janine asked Jeff several times if there was anything she could do for him, but each time, he refused. He whistled while he worked, loud enough for the sound to come in through the glass windows. Janine steamed in the car but didn't want to get out and stand strangely beside Jeff. She didn't want anyone to see her.

Suddenly, again out of nowhere, a cyclist ripped out from the crossroad and cycled toward the vehicle. It seemed like he'd wanted to stay on the wider shoulder, which wasn't on the other side of the road, but he hadn't expected to find a block. When his eyes spotted the vehicle and Jeff mending the tire behind it, they grew enormous, as wide as saucers.

His yelp rang out. He then yanked his bike to the right of the vehicle, narrowly missing Jeff. Because his action was so spontaneous, he lost his balance and tumbled into the grass along the side of the road.

"Oh my God!" Janine cried. She stepped out of the vehicle and found the poor guy in a heap on the ground, with his bike a few feet away from him. "Are you okay?"

Jeff jumped toward the man and extended a hand. The man looked up at him and blinked several times as he moaned. "Oomph. Just give me a minute."

The man unlatched his helmet and removed it as he tenderly lifted his back up from the ground. He assessed his legs as his dark hair swirled around his ears. They glowed with sweat.

"Man. I feel like a huge idiot," he said.

Jeff laughed. "I'm just glad you're okay! That could have ended a whole lot worse."

The man turned his head gingerly to peer up at Jeff. Now, Janine got a full view of his profile, his Roman nose, his full lips. With a jolt, she realized she actually knew this man. It wasn't a welcome feeling.

"Henry?" she said.

The man turned again to look at her, surprised. His eyes were bright with shock. "Oh. Janine." He cleared his throat as awkwardness folded between them. "Hi."

"You two know each other!" Jeff was exuberant as he helped Henry to his feet. "What a small world this is."

"Sure is," Janine said as she crossed her arms tightly over her chest. She felt suspicious in almost every way. It seemed like too much of a coincidence. "What brings you to Martha's Vineyard, Henry? Are you, um, working on a video project?"

She just couldn't trust him.

"Something like that," Henry told her. He looked on the verge of explaining himself. But instead, he stepped toward his bicycle and lifted it back to a standing position. "And yourself?"

"Just needed to get out of the city for a bit," Janine told him.

"Understandable."

Obviously, he knew all about the scandal and the affair and the drama that had unfolded at her apartment on the night of her daughter's engagement party. She struggled to remember if he'd actually been there that night. For a while, when Jack Potter had taken an interest in the documentary filmmaking of Henry Dawson, Jack and Henry had palled around together. "I've never met an artist like Henry," Jack had said, as he'd thrown more and more money at Henry's project. "His vision is something the world deserves to see."

But Janine reasoned she hadn't seen Henry since the

premiere of his most recent documentary, maybe two years before.

Henry returned his helmet to his head and gathered himself over his bike. He nodded toward Janine, then Jeff.

"Are you sure you're okay to cycle?" Jeff asked.

"Wasn't so bad, actually," Henry said. "Luckily, I'm pretty flexible."

Janine placed her hand over her throat. Dread permeated through her. "Hey Henry?" she said, just as he placed one of his feet on the pedal.

"Yes?"

"Please. Don't tell him where I am."

Henry furrowed his brow. He then placed his other foot on the pedal and cycled fast, away from Janine and Jeff. Janine's heart nearly burst in two. She realized she'd sounded like the craziest woman on the planet. Maybe she was.

Chapter Eight

The Katama Lodge and Wellness Spa was positioned along Katama Bay, the body of water that ballooned between Edgartown and the island of Chappaquiddick on the eastern skyline. Janine had investigated it on the map, but nothing fully prepared her for the sight of the lodge and spa itself — a large log cabin, with what looked to be four wings and four stories, with several balconies and porches that cut out toward the sandy beach beyond. Janine hovered outside the Katama Lodge vehicle as Jeff pulled out her suitcases.

"If you'd been here this time last year, you would have seen a bustling place. I'll tell you that. Women come from all over the world to stay here for weeks at a time. Talking to them was fascinating, as they were always from all walks of life, sometimes dealing with some major life change or medical issue. Of course, some came just to relax and be pampered like we all deserve."

Janine made a funny noise in her throat. She couldn't help but compare herself to these women and wondered if Jeff had said this purposely to allude to Janine's own heartache.

Of course, he really didn't seem to be that kind of guy. Cruelty had nothing to do with him.

"Yes. I really could always learn something about life or love or what it means to become older and wiser when I hung out here, driving Katama guests to and from the ferry and around the island," Jeff said as he placed his hands on his hips.

"But you don't think Nancy will reopen anytime soon?"

Jeff gave her a side-eyed glance, one that showed his curiosity at her calling her mother by her first name. "Like I said, Nancy and the girls are pretty broken up by Neal's death. I can't imagine it'll be an easy transition back. You have to be healed to heal others, I think."

"Who can say?" Janine returned, thinking again of the long-ago version of the Nancy she had known, who hadn't hesitated to pour herself a drink before three in the afternoon. Nancy — a healed Nancy, who could help heal others? It was difficult for Janine to imagine.

"There she is," Jeff beamed as a woman stepped out from the side of the lodge.

Janine's heart sank into her stomach as the woman came into view. She was trim and athletic, with a beautiful silver bob that bounced beneath her ears. She wore trendy clothing, including boot-cut jeans and a figure-hugging blouse. The woman gripped the wooden railing where she stood and looked out, her chin lifted.

Janine looked at her mother and couldn't believe how beautiful she looked — that her mother was so poised and confident in the way she held herself. Her memories of Nancy were far from what she saw right then and there, and Janine felt a pang of guilt from the last conversation she'd had with her mother over a decade ago.

But before another moment passed, Nancy's familiar laughter escaped her lips, and she called out, "Janine! You made it! I'll be right down."

Janine took several tentative steps forward as her mother raced to meet her. Janine's heart was in her throat, and her legs and arms quivered as though the weather wasn't balmy and warm. When Nancy appeared directly in front of her, she brought with her a wave of expensive-smelling perfume and that same, beautiful smile, the one that pulled Janine's heart, soul, and mind all the way back to Brooklyn in the '80s, when all she'd had was Nancy.

"Look at you," Nancy breathed as her eyes welled with tears.

Janine willed herself to remain hard. Her thoughts swirled in her head as she wrapped a strand of hair around her ear and turned her eyes back toward the Katama Lodge vehicle. "We had a flat tire on the way. Sorry if we're a bit late."

Nancy waved her hand back and forth. "Don't worry about it. My schedule is a whole lot looser these days. I guess Jeff filled you in a bit about how the Lodge has been closed for quite some time."

Janine furrowed her brow. *Was this her mother already asking for pity due to the death of her husband?* She searched for some sign of that in her eyes but found nothing but a strange mix of sorrow and eagerness for Janine's arrival.

"Do you also live here?" Janine asked.

Nancy shook her head. "We have a house about a mile from here. I just wanted to check on a few things this morning and make sure you saw the resort itself. I think it has a pretty stellar view of the Bay, although I might be biased."

Jeff announced that he would move the suitcases from the Katama Lodge vehicle over to Nancy's. Nancy thanked him and said she would need his help with some handiwork in a few days and that she would call him when she was ready to move forward. He thanked her profusely, then smiled at Janine as he said, "I hope you enjoy your stay here on the island. It's a one-of-a-kind place, and your mother is a one-of-a-kind person."

The words stung. As Jeff drew the vehicle back down the driveway, Janine wanted to rush after him, to scream at him that he had no idea what he was talking about. Nancy wasn't the woman, he thought he knew. But before she could, his vehicle disappeared.

She turned back to face her mother, who really did look somehow younger than she had twelve years before, the last time Janine had seen her in the city. That two- or three-hour meeting had been nothing short of disastrous. It had culminated in Janine's screaming at her mother to leave her apartment. *"I never want to see your face again,"* she'd cried as Maggie and Alyssa had escaped to their bedrooms, unable to fully comprehend the weight of the strange relationship between Nancy and Janine.

"Would you like to see the Lodge, then?" Nancy offered.

Janine supposed she didn't have a choice, so she shrugged and swept a hand out toward the log mansion. "Let's go."

Janine walked behind her mother as they entered the back of the building, which operated as the foyer and front desk area. A large photograph hung behind the desk, featuring Nancy alongside a man in his early seventies.

The man had a terrific smile, the stuff of early cinema, and his blue eyes glittered like the sky over Martha's Vineyard itself. Janine's heart dropped slowly as she realized that was the man her mother had loved and married. His name — Neal — hit her again. She would never know him.

"It's so terribly dark around here right now," Nancy said as she slid across the foyer and turned on a light. "It used to be that you'd stand in this room and hear echoes of countless conversations. Every person who came here had a story or two, and it seemed that everyone was constantly learning from one another, building friendships and communion."

Janine arched an eyebrow. Another sarcastic comment bubbled beneath the surface of her mind, but she refused to let it free.

"I actually started working here before Neal and I got together," Nancy said suddenly as she flashed a bit of her bob behind her shoulder and headed out of the foyer area toward a wraparound staircase.

Janine followed her up into a dining area with twenty-foot ceilings and windows that stretched floor-to-ceiling and offered a beautiful view of the water beyond. Tables stretched up and down the enormous room, and a window toward the back of the space showed an elaborate kitchen, the kind that could serve upward of fifty guests, maybe more, if Janine had to guess.

"I received my massage therapist license and began to work here part-time," Nancy continued. "Neal had just divorced his second wife, and he wasn't looking for anything serious. Heck, neither was I. I was something of a vagabond during those years. Always moving from place to place. I had it in my mind that I would never belong anywhere."

Ah. This was the Nancy that Janine understood. The drinking Nancy. The wild Nancy. The immature Nancy.

"But Neal, well, I guess you could say he changed my life." Nancy's eyes flashed as she said it.

Janine wanted to interject. She wanted to tell her mother that she couldn't just open up with her deep, personal emotions of her soul. Janine hadn't even begun to decide if she cared to forgive this woman yet.

In truth, Janine was just on the run from her mess of a life. She was only trying to find herself again.

When Janine didn't say anything to Nancy's "changed my life" comment, Nancy's shoulders slumped slightly, proof of her disappointment. But she hardly missed a beat. She beckoned for Janine to follow her from the dining area into the various other wings. She showed her where the acupuncture was performed, the sauna and spa, the hot tub, the cupping area along with the meditation area, and the space where they hired inspirational women to come and discuss what they'd learned. The lodge seemed somehow even bigger from the inside, and Janine found herself truly impressed, especially with the rustic-yet-chic décor and the fine artistic details, which made every room memorable.

"The women always report that they feel like they belong to some kind of club while they're here," Nancy said as they breezed past some of the larger suites, where women stayed the night. At the end of the hallway, they again enjoyed a beautiful view of Katama Bay, where the waves rolled in and splashed across the beach. Nancy went on to explain that all of their yoga sessions took place in the morning, poolside, before they continued on to a fully stacked schedule of activities. "Of course, I still don't know if we'll find a way to reopen."

Janine arched an eyebrow. She knew better than to pretend she truly cared about the state of this place. Her voice flat, she said, "And why is that?"

Nancy shrugged. "It's just a difficult thing, considering moving forward with the place without Neal. He was the heart and soul of this place."

"I see."

"His daughters helped us run it," Nancy explained as she turned back down the hallway and then entered a side staircase to lead Janine back to the foyer. "Elsa and Carmella. Elsa has taken her father's death particularly hard."

"And Carmella?"

Nancy's eyes flashed again. "Carmella handles things a bit differently. We all do, I suppose. Grief is a funny thing."

"Yes. It is." Janine held her mother's gaze for a moment as they both stirred in discomfort. There were thousands of things she could have thrown in her mother's face — regarding her abandonment of Janine and her horrible job of raising her.

But the woman who stood before Janine — this beautiful woman who now went by Nancy Remington, widow of Neal Remington — knew a far different reality than the one they had shared. Separately, Janine and Nancy had lived lives of luxury.

How strange.

"Well. I suppose that's all there is to see here for now," Nancy said softly as she shifted her weight on her white tennis shoes. "Elsa reports she's cooked us up a pretty big lunch. I hope you're hungry?"

Elsa. One of the stepdaughters. Janine's stepsister, who she'd only just learned about. Goose bumps popped up along Janine's arms and legs. Hunger was a very distant idea.

"That sounds good," Janine said. "Let's head over."

"Splendid." Nancy furrowed her brow, and her smile didn't match her eyes. "I want you to know that you're very welcome here, Janine, for as long as you want to be here. It means so much to me that you came."

Her words were powerful. They felt like a punch to the stomach.

"I'm sure I'll have to head back to the city sooner than later," Janine returned, her voice cold. "But I'm glad to see Martha's Vineyard, finally. So many of my friends over the years have recommended it. They all said the same thing that it's quite a magical place."

Her answer totally side-stepped the issue at hand. But there was no way she was going to acknowledge her complete meltdown and there was no way she was going to point to the fact that this was her and Nancy's first meeting in over a decade.

It was like they walked over a ravine, supported only by an unstable bridge. At any moment, that bridge might collapse and cast them to their deaths below. Forgiveness was maybe not possible. Maybe all they could do was live in whatever illusion they now created, especially after so much shared pain. Time would tell the tale.

Chapter Nine

Janine couldn't remember her mother behind the wheel of a car. She sat in the passenger seat and watched as the fifty-nine-year-old Nancy Remington pressed the button on her key chain, which roared up the engine of her BMW. It buzzed beneath them as she glanced into the rearview, then returned her eyes to the little camera beneath the radio, which gave a full view of the space behind the car.

"I always forget that's there," Nancy said as she eased her foot from the brake. "I told Neal it was so unnecessary. Humans have been driving for years and years without all this technology. But he told me once I had it, I'd never look back." Nancy flashed her eyes toward Janine as a laugh escaped her lips. "Get it? I'll never look back? Neal was always so witty. Gosh, I wish you could have met him."

Janine wasn't sure what to say. When they reached the road, Nancy pulled out and started their drive. She splayed her hand toward the Katama Lodge and heaved a sigh. "I'm glad you got to see the place. Maybe you can

70

help me and Elsa decide what's next. We could always sell it. Ah, but imagining someone else storming in and redesigning everything... it hurts just to think about."

Neal Remington's family home was located on the waterline, southwest of the city of Edgartown and the Katama Lodge, near Katama Beach, and very close to the Katama Airport. It was a dusty rose color, with large windows and a porch that wrapped around the front and the back. The place was wholesome and large; the type of place that you could tell brimmed with countless memories and should have been stocked with children, laughter, animals, and life. From the driveway, however, Janine sensed nothing of the kind. It seemed the house once had a life; now, it was in some kind of retirement.

"This is the place," Nancy said softly. These were the first words in several minutes, and they seemed so simple yet so profound.

"It's beautiful," Janine said, surprising herself.

"Thank you for saying that." Nancy tilted her head as she turned off the engine. "I sometimes pinch myself when I look at it. When Neal first brought me here, I wanted to tell him. You know—everything."

Janine furrowed her brow. She had a hunch about what her mother referred to — the multiple slum apartments they'd lived in, the countless nights they'd spent without much food. These were stories she didn't want to get into or think about.

"But instead, I just let it happen to me. I followed him inside that door, and I just knew that we would live a beautiful life together. And we did, for ten full years."

They gathered Janine's two suitcases from the trunk just as Nancy commented, "I'm surprised you don't have more luggage?"

To this, Janine could only say, "I just grabbed what I could and got out."

Nancy seemed unwilling to touch that subject.

They continued to dance around what they could say and what they couldn't say, like that children's game where you pretend that the carpet is lava.

When they reached the front door, Nancy opened it promptly, without the use of a key, and said, "It isn't like the city here. People just don't lock up as often. It took me years to get used to it, but now, I can't believe I lived any other way."

Buttery and herb smells wafted out from what she assumed would be the kitchen. Janine placed her suitcases in the foyer and removed her heels, which had begun to make her feet swell. When she glanced up from her bright red toes, she found a woman standing between the kitchen and the foyer, wearing an anxious smile. Her eyes were midnight blue, and her smile was large, the stuff of toothpaste commercials or State Fair queens. She looked at Janine with endless curiosity and then held up a spatula as she greeted with a smile. "You must be Janine."

Nancy drew her palms together and beamed at both of them. "Janine, this is my darling stepdaughter, Elsa. And yes, Elsa, this is my daughter. Janine Potter."

Janine shivered at the use of Jack's last name, even though it had been her own for over twenty years. She held Elsa's gaze as she stepped toward her and shook her hand. It seemed foolish to shake the hand of her new "step-sister," but a hug seemed even more foolish considering the situation. Besides, she didn't want Elsa to think she was ready to full-on accept her mother's adopted life.

"I'm so glad you made it," Elsa said. She was soft-spoken, or else just shy, and she held Janine's eyes without aggression. All she could sense was warmth.

This was a woman who knew a very, very different version of Nancy. Janine's stomach soured as she considered what Elsa might know already about Janine. What had Nancy told her? What story did she have?

"How's the cooking going?" Nancy asked after a long pause.

"Almost done!" Elsa replied. She dropped Janine's hand and beckoned for them to follow her. Once in the kitchen, she showed them the elaborate seafood meal she'd prepared, complete with crab, salmon, and buttery biscuits with marbled cheese throughout. Already, she'd set the table on the back porch, which overlooked the glittering water, and now, she popped open a chilled bottle of chardonnay.

Janine glanced toward her mother, suddenly panicked. After all, her mother around alcohol didn't bring back particularly stellar memories. But steadily, Nancy poured them each moderately-sized glasses and then lifted hers to say, "A toast to having my daughter home with me. What a remarkable blessing it is."

Janine's cheeks grew crimson. Without making eye contact, she clinked her glass with her mother's, then took a small sip. Her mother sipped as well, rather than downing it like she used to back in the day. Janine wondered just how much Nancy had changed. What was she all about?

The three of them gathered around the table outside. From there, the sound of the waves rushed through the salty air, and Janine felt her shoulders loosen just the slightest bit. There was certain calmness, a sereneness to the view. For a moment, as she gazed out at the horizon, she could pretend that this wasn't one of the strangest days of her life.

The food was delicious. Janine ate slowly, savoring each flavor that rolled over her palate.

"It's really incredible, Elsa," she complimented after a few bites. "I don't think I've had seafood like this ever in my life."

"Thank you. The restaurants around here make some delicious seafood dishes, but I've always loved making my own," Elsa said with a smile. "But it also helps that the seafood is fresh off the boats, so the dishes taste as fresh as they can get."

Janine sipped a bit of her chardonnay. "Have you spent much time in the city?"

"I went there on trips with my husband," Elsa told her. "He loved it and sometimes even talked about moving there. I always told him he could go without me. The Vineyard has always been my home."

As Elsa said it, her eyes flashed the slightest bit of sadness. Janine furrowed her brow.

"Where do you live on the island?" she asked. It was better to make small talk, maybe.

"My husband and I raised our children not far from here," Elsa told her. "Three of them. Cole, Mallory, and Alexie. Alexie's away at NYU, actually. Her father was so proud of her for that."

Janine's heart bulged slightly at the use of the past tense. She sensed a horrible story.

"But I've stayed here the past year or so," Elsa continued. Her voice broke slightly. "I grew up in this house, and it seemed fitting to come here after my husband died."

Janine pressed her lips together. The devastation hit her like a wave. "I am so sorry to hear that, Elsa. Really."

Elsa gave a light shrug. "Cancer. Nothing you can do when it chooses you, sometimes."

Nancy reached across the table and gripped Elsa's hand. Her own eyes were now rimmed with tears. "We've had a hell of a year, haven't we, Elsa?"

Elsa's voice broke. "Your mom has been there for me in every way."

"And Elsa's been there for me," Nancy affirmed. "We both lost so much this year."

Janine turned her eyes toward her uneaten crab. She suddenly felt horribly exposed and strange. Yes — her best friend in the world and her husband had had an affair, and she now felt cast out from her life of luxury. But other people had problems as well, much bigger issues.

Worst of all, other people had people to lean on. Nancy Remington had Elsa; Elsa had Nancy.

Janine felt like a stranger— a daughter who didn't exist. Now, she looked at the woman who filled her spot. And, honestly, she didn't know how to feel about that. It was clear to her, from the look Nancy gave Elsa now, that Elsa and Nancy's relationship was stronger than Nancy and Janine's had ever been. She imagined them sitting at that very table, late into the night, speaking and sharing their most important thoughts and secrets.

What was this feeling? Jealousy? Anger? Whatever it was, Janine wasn't sure what to do with it.

"And now, your mother has mentioned that you might be — well," Elsa furrowed her brow as she dropped her eyes to the table.

"Getting divorced?" Janine interjected. Shame fell

over her shoulders. "I guess so. Yes." She swallowed another bite of crab as silence enveloped them.

Finally, she said, "The Lodge is quite something. Nancy took me on a tour when I arrived earlier."

Elsa's eyebrows raised high on her forehead, probably at Janine's calling her mother by her first name. After a beat, Elsa said, "Dad and Nancy and I did everything for that place. It's our life."

"I can see why," Janine returned.

"I do miss it." Elsa studied the waterline, deep in thought. "But I just don't know how we could ever return to it. Dad was the driving force behind everything we did. His death was such a surprise. Sure, he'd had a few health problems, but I thought, we thought —"

"We definitely thought we had many more years together," Nancy affirmed tenderly.

After dinner, Janine helped wash the plates, pots, and pans. Elsa then led her to her bedroom, on the second floor, with a large window that overlooked the water and an en suite bathroom. It was still only late afternoon, but Janine confessed she was exhausted and wanted to take a few hours to herself. Elsa looked hesitant, as though she wanted to say something to make up for the awkwardness between them.

Finally, she mustered, "Your mother is really something special. She's been my saving grace."

Janine gave a slight shrug. Before she knew it, she blurted out, "It's pretty difficult for me to imagine that, to be honest."

Elsa's eyes grew shadowed. She studied Janine's face for a long moment, then stepped back into the hallway. She seemed to want to say a million things but didn't know where to start.

"Let me know if you need anything at all or if you want to borrow the car or anything. Our home is your home for as long as you want it. Nancy has said this over and over again since you agreed to come."

Janine's heart felt wounded. How desperately she wanted to explain herself — and all the bad blood she and Nancy had together. But Elsa was just a stranger, and there was no way she would understand. Besides, it didn't concern her.

"Thank you," she said instead as she slowly closed the door.

Once alone, Janine called her eldest daughter. Maggie answered on the second ring, and her voice was high-pitched as though she prepared for the worst.

"Hi, Mom. Did you meet her? How is everything?"

Janine sat at the edge of her bed and blinked out toward the ocean. "Everything is good, and yes, honey, I did."

"And? What's she like now?"

Janine hardly had the words due to her own confusion. "I don't know. It's like she walked out of a Martha Stewart catalog. She kind of looks like my mother and talks like my mother, but she also looks and acts like a very rich Martha's Vineyard housewife too."

"Huh. Well. She did marry that guy."

"But can a single marriage change your entire personality?"

"I don't know." Maggie sounded doubtful. "You don't sound happy."

"I think I'm just really confused," Janine answered. "Maybe I made a mistake by coming here. Nancy and I haven't gotten along in decades. There's so much pain between us. I'm not sure how we can overcome it. And I'm dealing with my own issues right now."

Maggie held the silence for a long time. Finally, she exhaled and said, "Mom, imagine if you and I had a rift between us. You would do anything to fix it. Maybe that's what Nancy is doing now. I know I would do anything in my power to heal my relationship with my daughter if I had one. You have to give her a chance, Mom. I'm sure she loves you so much and regrets the past. Plus, this will keep your mind off Dad. You need to focus on you right now."

Janine's heart lifted. "Maggie, don't be silly. We would never have a rift between us. And when did you become so wise?"

Maggie breathed in the other end of the phone as a sign of resignation.

"All right, honey. Everything you've said makes so much sense. I'm just going to take it one day at a time. I'll keep you in the loop."

"I love you, Mom," Maggie said. "Oh, and Mom?"

"Yes?"

"You're the strongest woman I know. Never forget that. You've got this."

Chapter Ten

Janine had insomnia quite frequently. This was a very common ailment in New York City with the stress and the traffic and the constant feeling of existential dread, which people seemed to wear along with their designer jewelry. Janine had a prescription for sleeping pills, but Jack had told her he didn't like the way they made her so groggy in the mornings, and they'd caused her to sleepwalk a few times and whisper in her sleep. Of course, he'd always had his backup bedroom to leave her alone in her anxious thoughts, going in and out of slumber.

At around five thirty in the morning, as the soft light of the morning streamed through the window, Janine gave up on getting back to dreamland. She placed her feet on the hardwood floors and stretched her arms over her head. Her eyes flirted with her cell phone, there on the nightstand, and her brain itched for her to search up the various gossip sites and see if anyone had reported her abandonment of the city. Seeing Henry, the documentary filmmaker, had put a jolt in her plans, as she'd wanted to be invisible to her old life, as though she no longer existed.

Janine had unpacked and hung all her garments in the closet. This was something she'd grown accustomed to doing, regardless of how long she planned to stay in a place, as it made her feel more grounded. She'd considered the fact that maybe since she and her mother had had to move around so much when she'd been a kid, this unpacking was a direct assault against her memories. It was a way to say, *No, I will stay around, thank you very much*—a way to exert control.

Janine didn't have much in the way of "casual clothing." She flipped through her dresses and pantsuits before she discovered a pair of designer jeans, which she tugged up over her hips. She then added a sweater, which had been knitted in Belgium, and glanced at herself in the mirror. Her face was barren of makeup, and big craters swirled beneath her eyes. If her New York friends saw her like this, they might use the words "having a nervous breakdown" to describe her.

Downstairs, Janine found that a coffee pot had been brewed, but nobody sat in any traditional coffee-drinking locations to sip it. She poured herself a mug and stepped out onto the porch. The sea breeze fluttered through her hair and cooled her cheeks, and she closed her eyes somberly and listened to the gentle rush of the waves. She was reminded of all the artists of the 19th century, who'd been sent to "the seaside" to mend their health. Maybe this was meant for her.

When she finished her cup of coffee, Janine felt vibrant, like a renewed sense of energy swept over her.

She stepped off the porch and wandered down to the sand, where she slipped out of her shoes and rolled up her jeans. The water was chilly but not frigid, and it frothed around her ankles. She continued to walk, her feet in the water, and she lost herself in the meditative nature of it all, the sea and the cawing birds and the boats, far out in the distance, as they made their somber journeys elsewhere.

Janine returned to the house around seven in the morning. The thought of indoors was ridiculous to her when the air tasted so fresh and tart, but she walked inside anyway to search for a book upstairs. When she returned to the veranda, she slid into the cushioned porch swing and dug into the words hungrily. When was the last time she'd given herself time and space to read?

But very quickly, her focus ran dry.

It wasn't for lack of trying. Inside the house, a door slammed, and she heard Elsa's voice. "Good morning." The words didn't sound welcoming. They were flat, and they seemed to build a boundary.

The response of, "Hey," wasn't so kind, either. Janine didn't recognize the voice. She sat straight upright, her book still on her lap.

"Didn't expect you so early," Elsa said. "I'll pour you some coffee."

"Thanks."

The voices carried into the kitchen, just on the other side of the nearest window to Janine. There was the sound of the coffee being poured, then Elsa asked the other woman, "Are you still vegan? I only have cow milk."

"Black is fine."

"You're making sure all your levels are okay with that

vegan stuff, aren't you? I worry you won't get all the right nutrients," Elsa returned.

"Millions of people are vegan, Elsa. And I told you. I only do the vegan thing a few times a week."

"Which days?"

"Elsa, stop nagging," the other woman said. She then cleared her throat and lowered her voice. "So have you met her. Nancy's daughter?"

There was silence. Janine could practically feel Elsa's nod.

"And? How is she?" the other woman asked.

Elsa paused for a long time before she answered. "She just seems sad."

"Huh. Well. Join the club, I guess," the other woman remarked dryly.

"Carmella, come on."

Ah. So this woman was Carmella, Elsa's sister and Nancy's second stepdaughter. The one who hadn't shown up the previous night and the one Nancy had alluded was a bit emotional, a bit different.

"What do you mean, come on? Every time I walk in this house, I feel like I'm walking into a funeral home," Carmella returned.

"Nancy and I are helping each other get through," Elsa said tentatively.

"And how much longer will it take for you to get through?" Carmella asked. "I need to get my acupuncture practice up and running again. I'm going crazy."

"We need to hire a new overall wellness specialist," Elsa returned. "You know that."

"And you haven't interviewed a single person for the job," Carmella pointed out. "And meanwhile, the Lodge is just empty. What do you think Dad would think of that?"

"Like you honestly care what Dad would think," Elsa bristled.

Again, silence. Janine had never had a sister, although she did remember the few spats she'd had with Maxine (non-blood related, yet ever a sister, until recently). It had always seemed like, because they'd known one another so well, they'd known precisely what to say to dig the knife in.

"Come on, Elsa. You don't have the trademark for being sad about Dad's death," Carmella returned icily.

"My husband died too, you know."

This time, Carmella didn't respond. Janine's eyes grew watery as she realized she'd forgotten to blink.

Finally, Elsa spoke again. "I swear, Carmella. Your lack of empathy is really astounding, sometimes. It feels like Karen never really left."

Carmella cackled at that. "You love bringing that up, don't you?"

It was strange to witness this from the other side of the window. Janine felt as though she was at the top of a mountain, peering down at a vast valley of family drama. It was never easy to comprehend the weight of other people's stories.

There was a soft sob. It sounded like it came from Elsa, although Janine couldn't be sure.

"Off to a great start today, aren't we, Carmella?" Elsa breathed between cries.

Carmella grumbled. Clearly, she wasn't the kind of woman to cry. After a long pause, she said, "Here. Mop yourself up."

Janine could imagine her bringing a packet of tissue

from her purse. She could imagine Elsa taking one. Then she heard the soft blowing of her nose.

Finally, Carmella heaved a sigh. "If you don't want to start back up the Lodge for now, then fine. I have a number of acupuncture clients who need appointments; therefore, I'll use my space. Otherwise, they might find another acupuncturist." She paused again. "You don't want me to lose my clients, do you?"

"Of course not," Elsa whispered.

"Fine. Okay. Pass this news along to Nancy, will you?"

"Okay."

Then there was the sound of Carmella's heels making a clacking sound as she walked out of the kitchen and back toward the front door. Janine shivered and then busied herself with a heavy prayer in the hopes that Elsa wouldn't pick this moment to head out onto the veranda and discover her. Thankfully, she didn't.

Who was Karen? Why didn't Carmella seem to care as much about the death of their father as Elsa? What was this strange rift between sisters?

Suddenly, something caught Janine's attention, and she whipped around to find a horse, moving slowly toward her, down the beach. Atop the black beauty was her mother, Nancy, wearing a riding cap and a beautiful burgundy riding cape. Janine had never seen her mother on horseback before. Slowly, she stood and lifted her hand in greeting. Her mother turned the horse evenly toward her, and her grin widened as she approached.

Janine felt like a huge sap. She was strangely reminded of being a little kid, maybe four or five, and spotting her mother as she entered preschool to pick her up for the day. It had been the best moment of the day, every single day, during a very, very finite portion of Janine's life.

Nancy slid off the horse with ease and wrapped the reins around her fingers as she approached the porch.

"Look at you," Janine said as she placed her hands on the porch railing.

"I like to get a ride in early in the morning," Nancy told her.

Again, there was this bubble of awkwardness between them, as though they would never find ways to tell each other exactly what lurked on their minds.

"Jack and I used to ride in California," Janine said suddenly as the memory passed through her. "Jack was really seasoned, and he showed me some techniques."

"Maybe we can go together sometime," Nancy offered. "We have four horses. It was one of Neal's passions."

"These men in our lives and their love of horses," Janine said, her voice breaking.

Beneath the surface, there was the memory of a time when the idea of Janine and Nancy riding a horse would have been preposterous. Beyond that, neither Jack nor Neal was in their lives at the moment. It was just them.

"I'll take him back to the stables," Nancy said after a pause. "Then maybe some breakfast and a surprise."

"A surprise?" Janine arched her eyebrow.

Nancy nodded. "I like to do that now. Surprise people."

When Nancy disappeared, Janine returned to the kitchen, which was now void of Elsa and Carmella. She brewed another pot of coffee as her thoughts raced. Fear laced through her as she realized that she would maybe have to spend the next few hours with Nancy alone. The previous day, Elsa had been a buffer.

Janine had no idea how she would remain docile and even-keeled with Nancy. No matter how much time had passed, they couldn't avoid the darkness between them. It was ever-present.

Chapter Eleven

Janine found herself again in the passenger seat of Nancy's BMW. She folded and unfolded her hands on her lap as her mother twiddled with the radio stations and said, "How about classic rock?" just as she took her foot off the brake and pressed the gas, driving the car down the long driveway. Boston's "More Than A Feeling" buzzed from the speakers, and Janine tried to tell herself to breathe. This was her first official big day with her mother; the sun was shining, and the morning was fresh and light. Nothing could sour it. Maybe.

"Let's grab something sweet to eat," Nancy said, mostly to herself, as she whipped down the backroad and headed toward Edgartown. "What do you say to that?"

Janine gave a light shrug. "Okay."

Nancy flashed her eyes toward her daughter. "You used to beg me for donuts when you were little. Do you remember? You would pick up little coins from the sidewalk and try to add them together to make enough for a donut from the bakery. Once, you found two quarters, and you nearly lost your little mind because it meant you could have two donuts. One for me, and one for you."

Janine's heart dropped a bit. She could still remember the gooey delight of those donuts they'd purchased from an Italian immigrant's bakery on the corner of their block. She could still remember the way the bakery had smelled and how volatile the Italian baker had been when he'd been cranky, always yelling at his young son for taking donuts from the window.

Nancy parked the car outside a little rustic-looking bakery with a sign that read: Frosted Delights Bakery. Janine followed her mother inside to find a bustling cafe, with a friendly-looking and beautiful woman behind the counter. The woman had long, red tresses, and her fashion was spectacular, altogether wasted beneath her bakery apron.

"Nancy, hello!" the woman said.

"Jennifer, good to see you," Nancy returned warmly. "I told you I was on that diet and wouldn't be back for a while, remember?"

"I remember it all too well." Jennifer's laughter sparkled. "But I hear something like that from Vineyard residents about five times a day. I know better than to believe it. My mother's donut recipe is just too good."

"They're sinful," Nancy explained, her eyes connecting with Janine's. "Especially the frosted maple. Oh, but what was it you always loved as a girl?"

Janine watched, curious, as her mother's face twitched with the memory.

Finally, her mother snapped her fingers and said, "You liked caramel. And look. They have one there. Jennifer, we'll take one caramel and one maple, please."

"Coming right up," Jennifer affirmed.

Nancy gave Janine a look that said: *see? I wasn't the worst mother, was I? I remembered your favorite treat.*

And in truth, Janine was the slightest bit impressed.

"By the way, Jennifer, I want you to meet my daughter," Nancy said as Jennifer tapped the cost into the register. "This is Janine. She's here from the city. This is her first time on the island!"

Jennifer's lips formed a round O of surprise. "My gosh. I was going to say. She's the spitting image of you, Nancy. Really. Hi, Janine. Welcome to Martha's Vineyard. You should know that your mother is something of a pillar of our community around here."

Janine's cheek twitched as she took the bag of donuts from Jennifer. *A pillar of the community? Her mother? Nancy?* And there it was again — that constant "you look just like twins!" refrain.

"I'm happy to be here," Janine said, her voice strained.

"We have a big day planned," Nancy told Jennifer.

"I should think so. How do you show Martha's Vineyard for the first time? Especially to someone so important." Jennifer's smile grew wider.

But Janine's stomach clenched with resentment. *This woman? Did she really think she knew Nancy Grimson?* Janine had a few stories that would enlighten her.

Back outside, Nancy said, "Let's stretch our legs the rest of the way. Do you mind?"

"We'll just leave your car here at the bakery?"

"It's a pretty safe little place," Nancy said. "Like I said. We hardly ever lock our doors. We hardly ever worry about anything, really. After Brooklyn and that year I spent in Bangkok — it's such a relief."

Janine stopped short and gave her mother a bug-eyed look. "Bangkok?"

Nancy's lips quivered into a smile. "I suppose you don't know. That's where I went that year after I visited you last in New York. I got my massage therapist license there and practiced for a number of months."

"In Thailand?" Janine was incredulous.

"It's part of the reason I got the job at the Katama Lodge," Nancy said. "Neal was there on business."

"You met Neal in Bangkok?" Janine demanded.

"Yes. But we didn't get together until later. Although I have to admit, sparks flew the minute I saw him. At least for me."

Janine felt more and more like her mother was a complete stranger.

Nancy led Janine toward the Edgartown Harbor, where a number of sailboats rested up against the docks and swayed with the breeze. When they reached the edge of the dock, Nancy waved a hand through the air, and another arm in the distance waved back. As the boat approached, Janine recognized its sailor as Jeff, the man she had met the previous day.

Just before the boat made its way up to the dock, Nancy said, "I want you to experience the island in the most beautiful way, which is from the water. At least, that's my opinion." She paused and then asked, "Have you been on a sailboat before?"

Janine had. She and Jack had chartered a sailboat in Greece when Alyssa and Maggie had been ten and eight. They'd stayed with babysitters in Athens while Janine and Jack had floated from island to island.

But Janine didn't want to dwell in the past.

"A few times," Janine said. "But it's been a while."

"Of course you have," Nancy said. "I have a feeling your experiences would fill many different memoirs, now."

"With the marvelous conclusion of my husband's affair," Janine interjected, almost without realizing the words spewed out.

But before Nancy could respond, Jeff latched to the side and then helped the two of them onto the teetering boat. He beamed at them and said, "When Nancy suggested we take you out sailing today, I knew it was the perfect way to greet you. You don't get seasick, do you?"

Janine, whose stomach now swirled around strangely, maybe due to the donut or the memories that flung through her, said, "No. I've never gotten seasick."

Of course, there was a first time for everything.

Janine settled herself on a little chair, which was attached to the side of the boat. The sails flourished out as the sea air rushed through them, and in a matter of seconds, they pushed out from the docks and breezed north toward the Edgartown Lighthouse, located at the tip of a sandy beach, where light green grass swayed in the gentle June breeze. It was now close to nine in the morning, and tourists had begun to flock to the beaches and boardwalks; their bright white outfits glowed beneath the bright sun.

"It's really something to see the tourists come back," Nancy said softly.

"It must annoy you?" Janine asked.

"On the contrary," Nancy returned. "It's like renewed life back to the island. It's like the island flourishes again after very cold and dark winter nights. Oh, and this most previous winter was the worst of all." She exhaled again as her eyelashes fluttered across her cheeks. "I only wish

Neal could see this. It was his favorite time of year. End of spring, early summer — when days are both long and short and the entire world, it seems like, comes out to play on the Vineyard."

Janine allowed herself to acknowledge the beauty of the island as they swirled around it. They sailed westward, then up along the Joseph Sylvia State Beach, then they continued toward Oak Bluffs. Nancy explained that the two larger towns on the island were Oak Bluffs and Edgartown and that the island enjoyed a population of approximately 14,000 during the off-season.

"A tight-knit community," Nancy affirmed.

"It's definitely no Bangkok."

Nancy blushed. "You probably have some questions, don't you?"

Janine wasn't sure how to respond to that. Her stomach tightened.

But before she could say anything, Nancy said, "It's okay. I have some questions for you, too. I hope we'll find the time for each other."

Janine wasn't entirely sure she wanted that conversation to happen. She'd already nearly lost her mind over the story of the caramel donuts and the quarters found on the Brooklyn sidewalk. Digging deeper was dangerous. At least she thought so.

The sailing expedition lasted several hours. Jeff had packed them light snacks, including cheese and crackers, and freshly made bread he said he had purchased from the Sunrise Cove Inn Bistro's bakery.

"Christine always does such a good job," Nancy said as she sliced through the sourdough and paired a bit with some camembert. "Maybe you know her old restaurant, actually, Janine. She was the pastry chef for — oh, Jeff, what was Christine's old restaurant called? It was in Upper Manhattan. I'm sure of it."

Jeff snapped his fingers. "Wasn't it Chez something? Chez Frank?"

"That's it," Nancy squealed with delight. "A French place."

In fact, Janine did know it. It had been one of the more marvelous French cuisine restaurants in Upper Manhattan until it had spontaneously closed the previous summer. She'd heard a rumor that the owner had been a bit shady.

"It was delicious," she finally mustered, slightly hating that anything to do with her mother's life had aligned with hers back in Manhattan.

"You'll have to swing by the Sunrise Cove and meet Christine," Nancy suggested. "Although she does have her hands full these days. She's helping her niece raise her baby. Quite a family, the Sheridan clan. Oh — look! Janine, those cliffs are truly spectacular. Aquinnah Cliffs. Before you leave the island, we have to hike along them. It has the most beautiful views of the ocean."

Janine blinked up at the blissful tan stones and sands of the cliffs, which lined the western-most point of the island. She, too, took a little bite of the sourdough, which was sinfully delicious. By the time she'd finished her first slice, her mother had already prepared herself a second and dug in.

Look at us, she thought— feeling the breeze from the ocean and eating delicious foods without a care in the world. It was so strange how things worked, how time changed, how people changed.

How different it all was now compared to childhood and the worries that had surrounded them.

When they rounded back through Katama Bay, Nancy pointed out the Katama Lodge, where it lurked over the top of the water. Her eyes were glassy. "I miss that old place. Looks like a haunted lodge that hasn't been up and running in forever, doesn't it?"

Janine thought back to what Elsa had said that morning about Carmella's selfishness in wanting to reopen. It was a simple way to look at grief, saying you just needed to "get over it." Janine knew that well.

Several minutes before the docks came into view again, Janine's stomach jumped into her chest, then dropped again. Her intestines tried to tangle themselves up. She placed her hand over her gut and groaned.

"Honey, you look green," her mother said.

Janine's eyes snapped toward her mother's. *Why was she suddenly so angry? Did she just really not want to seem weak in front of her mother? Could it really be that simple?*

"I just need to get off this boat," Janine finally said through clenched teeth.

When they neared the dock, Janine lurched herself off the boat and hustled as far as she could away from the other sailors. Her legs were like jelly. When she couldn't run anymore, she fell to her knees and began to dry heave. She was no longer sure if it was seasickness or just the horror of her strange life that plagued her. She dry heaved again and almost willed something, anything to come out of her.

There was a hand on her upper back. Then there was her mother's voice.

"Honey? Are you okay?"

Janine snapped her head around, suddenly angry. "Honey?"

Nancy's face fell. "I'm sorry. I just—do you want water or something?"

Janine dry heaved again as Nancy removed her hand. "I just don't know why you think you can fix everything now," Janine muttered, mostly to the ground.

She knew the words were juvenile. She knew they wouldn't solve anything.

After a long silence, Janine forced herself back to her feet. She turned to look at her mother, whose eyes were filled with tears.

But then, something else caught her eye. Just beyond Nancy, stationed in a sailboat, was a video camera pointed directly at her. Janine bristled. She was reminded all over again of the gossip columnists and their obsession with her divorce and everything she'd had to endure. She glared at the camera for a long moment until the man behind it suddenly brought the camera down so he could check the shot he'd just taken.

The man behind the camera was Henry. The documentarian who was friends with Jack.

Mortified and totally enraged, Janine stormed toward his boat.

"Janine? What are you doing?" Nancy cried after her.

Henry didn't look up until Janine's arrival.

"What the hell do you think you're doing?" Janine demanded.

Henry's eyes lifted. His face fell in recognition. He'd been caught.

"Janine. Hello."

Janine resented this. "You can't just pretend you weren't videotaping me."

Henry balked. "What are you talking about, Janine? I wasn't."

Janine swept a hand out and beckoned for the camera. "Give me the camera. I want to delete it."

"I didn't take any video of you," Henry blared.

"That's such bull," Janine returned. "You're probably rough on money and know you can sell something like that to one of the tabloids. 'Jack Potter's ex has a nervous breakdown on Martha's Vineyard.' Blah, blah."

"You really think I — a multi-award-winning documentarian — would take any interest in some woman's mental decline?" Henry returned.

"Multi-award winning? Oh, wow. Love how you drop your accolades into the conversation, not that they mean anything." Janine scoffed. "As though any of your movies have ever made any money."

Henry's arms flailed back, then his eyes narrowed as he said, "Your husband let my last project die on the cutting room floor—"

Suddenly, in a quick, violent motion, he accidentally threw his video camera into the water. Janine's eyes went wide as the expensive black device went *THUNK* into the salty ocean. Henry blinked at the entry sight, too. They both seemed to ponder it with shock.

And Janine could imagine it as it floated through the glowing depths toward the ocean floor below.

Chapter Twelve

What Janine had said to Nancy in front of the Edgartown Lighthouse seemed to put a wedge between the two of them for the rest of the day. In some respects, Janine felt guilty, as she knew her mother had only tried to create a beautiful memory of the two of them — trying to find a way to bridge beyond the sadness. It had resulted in near vomit, a dead video camera, and a very quiet car ride back to Nancy's house, where Janine drew herself a steaming bath and stared at the white glow of the wall for a good hour while hardly focusing on anything.

Elsa came to her room around three thirty and asked if she wanted to go for a walk or head to the fish market over by Oak Bluffs. Janine tried to lend a smile but couldn't feel it in her eyes. Elsa's own fake smile dropped, too.

"I don't think I'm up for it. The sailing took a lot out of me," Janine told her.

"Yeah. I understand that," Elsa returned. "Nancy said you got a bit seasick?"

"Something like that."

"I'll make you something easy on the stomach for dinner," Elsa said. "Soup or something."

"You don't need to do that." If she was honest, she wasn't sure she wanted to eat anything for the rest of the day.

"Nonsense. That's the kind of thing we do around here," Elsa replied evenly. "We take care of each other."

Janine wrapped herself up in a robe and fell back on the bed. She'd entered back into dark-gloomy-depressed Janine, and she wasn't sure how to yank herself out of it. She scanned through her phone, grateful that the gossip columnists had focused on a few other Manhattan celebrities that day. Perhaps they would move on from her for good. After all, she wasn't Jack Potter's wife any longer.

At the end of one of the articles, she spotted clickbait for something else: **MAXINE AUBERT STEPS OUT IN PUBLIC WITH JACK POTTER FOR FIRST TIME.**

Don't click, Janine told herself. *Don't you dare click.*

But of course, she clicked. How could she not?

Suddenly, she found herself staring at a photograph of the two people she loved more than any others in the world. Maxine wore six-inch heels and a long skirt, with a slice up the side that highlighted her absolutely iconic legs. She wore a jean jacket, which made her look youthful, and her hair was tousled beautifully. Jack wore a button-down and a pair of jeans, and he had his hands in his pockets while Maxine wrapped her hand around his bicep and spoke to him about something.

The first line of the article was this: **Finally,**

Maxine Aubert breathes a sigh of relief as her love is finally allowed to flourish in public.

Janine thought she might dry-heave all over again.

That moment, as though God himself knew she needed help, Alyssa texted.

> ALYSSA: Hey, Mom! How's that island?
> And Grandma?

> JANINE: Hey, honey. It's pretty beautiful.

She sent along a few shots she'd taken that morning of the island from the sailboat. It was a funny thing how bad photos were at capturing reality. Each glowing photograph was a representation of Janine's most heartbroken moments.

> ALYSSA: Wow! It looks so beautiful.

> JANINE: How are you doing?

> ALYSSA: You didn't answer about
> Grandma. Ha ha. How is she?

> JANINE: She looks like a supermodel. I
> should have known she would rebound.

> JANINE: And apparently, she lived in
> Thailand for a full year.

> ALYSSA: What? She's such a surprise.

> JANINE: True.

> ALYSSA: Maybe I could come to the island to meet her? It's been twelve years since the last time, so I don't remember her that well.

Janine pondered this. After a long pause, she wrote back.

> JANINE: Maybe.

For reasons she wasn't entirely sure of, she kind of wanted to keep her "real" loves, Maggie and Alyssa, from this strange poison that lurked between herself and Nancy. It seemed bad luck to join her two worlds together.

* * *

Janine kept a low profile for the next few days. She enjoyed occasional lunches and dinners with Elsa and Nancy, who seemed to always have something to say to one another — the perfect mother-daughter combo. Then Janine either walked the beach, or went jogging, or swam in the salty waters. She read her book, found a local bookstore to purchase even more books, and started to try to write out a list of possible options for the rest of her life.

After all, she'd come to the island to hide and to heal and to think. The sooner she figured out what to do next, the better off she was.

And, of course, a text from Jack stating that he needed an address to send out the divorce papers didn't exactly thrill her.

At the top of the list, she wrote:

THINGS TO DO WITH THE REST OF MY LIFE

1. Remember what it was you liked to do before you were rich.

But what was that, exactly? Janine had been "rich" since age nineteen when she'd given birth to Maggie, who was the heir to Jack Potter's fortune. She still remembered the first taste of caviar, the first thousand-dollar bottle of champagne, the first private jet. All that had fallen down upon her, and she'd reveled in it.

And then, of course, it had just been commonplace. It had been like the weather.

When Janine had been twenty-eight, she'd had something of a crisis. She had hardly spoken with Jack about it, as she hadn't wanted to bother him. But she had talked about it extensively with Maxine, who'd helped her come to the conclusion that she needed to do something with her time that wasn't affiliated with being a "Manhattan socialite" and "care for the children."

This had led Janine to pave her path toward becoming a respected naturopathic doctor among her peers.

At first, Jack said it wasn't medicine, or they were quacks. Then she'd treated him holistically for his back pain, and he hadn't said a bad word since. After Janine had begun her own practice, she'd lined up a number of clients, all of whom returned to her week after week, month after month. She was once written up in a naturopathic medicine magazine. The memory of that still thrilled her. Seeing her standing in her own spotlight enthralled her. Janine was no longer in her husband's limelight as the wife of a rich socialite. She'd earned her own accolades and was proud of that.

But two years prior, Janine had closed up her practice. She'd set aside her love of naturopathic medicine, passed on her clients to others, and busied herself with her Manhattan social scene and her supposedly loving husband. Deep down, she wasn't sure if Jack resented her for going out on her own and achieving such a large goal, which most of the other wives never did or even attempted. At the time, she'd told herself she'd finished with naturopathic medicine. But now that she thought back, the origin of her departure was rooted to a particularly strange exchange she'd had with one of Jack's friend's wives. "I could never work outside the home," she'd said. "I need to make sure I dote on my husband. I know that if I don't, someone else will."

Janine had told herself at the time that she hadn't left her practice for Jack or for anyone.

Now, she wasn't so sure.

Toward the end of her first week, Janine slipped out of her bedroom and made her way downstairs. She found the kitchen empty, sparkling clean as ever, and neither Elsa nor her mother's vehicles were in the driveway. She was grateful to have the place to herself, but even as she sat at the kitchen table and peered out at the gray and cloudy afternoon, her soul felt anxious. Without thinking, she rushed to the closet, grabbed her coat, pushed her feet into tennis shoes, and then headed out the door.

Janine walked east along the Atlantic Ocean until the waterline cut north into the Bay. As weather threatened rain, and there was a chill to the air, the beaches were largely empty, and she enjoyed her ability to march directly across the sand as though she ruled the island.

She listened to nothing on her headphones and the sound of the waves rolled in fast due to the frantic winds.

When she stood at the edge of the waters, she tried to call Maggie. When Maggie didn't answer, she tried Alyssa. Both of her girls were out in the world, doing their best to be a part of it. Janine was in hiding. She wondered what they thought of that. She hoped they understood — that she felt broken, and she wasn't entirely sure how to put herself back together.

When she reached the Katama Lodge and Wellness Spa, she stopped short, surprised she'd walked so far. The place looked much more enormous from the beach. The curtains had been drawn over the windows, which gave it a strange, haunted feel. In fact, Janine might have passed right on by had she not noticed a dark blue vehicle that snaked up the driveway and parked on the far end of the Lodge itself.

Then there was the screech of a door opening, which led out onto the porch that overlooked the water. Not wanting to be caught gawking, Janine jumped around the side and back toward the front entrance, which led in from the driveway. Once there, she watched as the driver of the blue vehicle marched in, her hair in a ponytail. It whipped around behind her as she entered.

Curious, Janine followed the woman into the foyer. Once there, she found herself in a bustling foyer with Carmella, the stepsister she hadn't met yet, at the front desk. The woman in the ponytail was checking in, and three other women were seated in chairs, waiting for appointments. Soft light streamed in through a door in the distance, as did a number of friendly female voices.

Janine was reminded of a club she'd belonged to back in New York City — an exclusive one for rich families, which had filled with beautiful women throughout the afternoons and early evenings. Although Janine had spent quite a bit of time there, she'd never felt such warmth coming from the space, not like here.

In fact, even as she stood there, Carmella lifted her beautiful eyes and said, "Good afternoon. Welcome to Katama Lodge and Wellness Spa. I'll be with you in a second."

"Thank you," Janine replied.

Of course, Carmella had no idea that she was Janine. This meant Janine could introduce herself.

Although, wasn't that kind of weird, especially since it seemed like Carmella and Nancy and Elsa didn't all get along?

When Carmella finished checking in the woman with the ponytail, she turned her full attention to Janine. "Do you have an appointment?"

"I don't, actually."

"Oh, oh no. I'm sorry to say that I'm pretty booked this week," Carmella said.

"What about the rest of the lodge and spa?" Janine asked.

"Unfortunately, we're only running our acupuncturist clinic right now." Carmella furrowed her brow. "I hope we'll have the lodge and spa back up and running by the end of the summer, but there's no way to know."

"That's too bad," Janine offered.

"It really is. I miss it." Carmella paused for a moment and then tilted her head out toward the hallway, which led to the beautiful, simmering voices. "Listen. We have some cucumber water, smoothies, and margaritas out on the back porch. A few of the girls who've already had their sessions for the day stuck around to hang out. You can join them if you want to. Sometimes I think that's what I miss most about this place—the communion."

Janine walked tentatively toward the voices to find a covered porch with six beautiful women, all wearing fuzzy robes and drinking cocktails, bubbly waters, or some of both. A woman with long, sleek dark hair turned her head languidly toward Janine and delivered a relaxed smile.

"Hello there. Did Carmella just poke you?"

Janine laughed. "No. She's booked. I'm just checking out the space."

"Oh, you have to sit with us," another girl, blond, said as she tapped the closest chair. "Have a margarita. Mila makes them about as strong as ever. Unfortunately, Amelia can't drink them."

The woman, who was clearly named Amelia, scrunched her nose and said, "Pregnant," with a funny shrug.

"Ah." Janine nodded as she slid into the chair next to the blond woman. The pregnant Amelia seemed maybe around her own age, which surprised her. She was grateful she didn't have to birth babies any longer. Those painful days and sleepless nights were far, far in the past.

Someone handed her a margarita, which she sipped slowly as the women around her fell into conversation again. It wasn't for another few minutes, when one of them pressed her on the knee, that she fully realized that they'd asked her a question.

"What brings you here?" the woman with the sleek, brown tresses asked.

Janine parted her lips with surprise. "What do you mean?"

The woman giggled and lifted her margarita. "Apologies for the forward question. It's just — you seem like it's your first time at the Katama Lodge. Most of us end up here for a reason. Like me. A few years back, my husband died unexpectedly."

"Oh. I'm so sorry to hear that," Janine breathed.

The woman nodded. "It was a terrible time. I have twins, but luckily, my good friends here cared for them for a few days while I checked in here. Nancy, Neal, Carmella, and Elsa were all so kind to me during that time. I really regained my strength."

Janine felt, again, the strangeness of being told what a remarkable woman her mother, Nancy, was.

"We all felt so heartsick when Neal died," Amelia said. "We know how much Nancy loved him. He was such a good man."

"And how much Neal loved Nancy," the woman with the dark hair said.

"I don't blame her for closing down for a bit," the blond woman murmured. "And Elsa is a wreck, too. I saw her out with her grandbaby recently. She carried him and cried and — well. It just about broke my heart."

Janine's heart sank.

"What do you think Elsa thinks of Carmella reopening the acupuncture area?" Amelia whispered.

"I don't know," the blond woman said. "But you know there's all that bad blood between them. I have a hunch they bickered about it."

"Nancy tries to stay out of it," the woman with the dark hair said. "Oh, but I wish she knew how much this place helps all of us. I feel totally at peace here. Like I can breathe again."

The other women agreed as the blond woman turned

toward Janine and said, "I'm sorry. My friend, Mila here, forgot she asked you a question."

"Oh. Right. What brings me here," Janine repeated.

The women turned their complete focus toward Janine. They were honest and open and curious — but there was none of that Manhattan malice, which Janine had grown accustomed to over the years.

"Well. I mean, it's the age-old story, isn't it?" Janine whispered. "I'm getting divorced. I've lost my way. I'm just not really sure who I am anymore."

The women nodded. Some of them closed their eyes and muttered, "I understand completely."

It was a safe space. It was a place to forget and heal.

Janine sipped her margarita.

Maybe her mother's world wasn't so venomous, after all.

Chapter Thirteen

When Janine arrived home from the Katama Lodge and Wellness Spa, she found her mother dressed in a summer dress, hovering at the hallway mirror, dotting lipstick tenderly across her lips. Janine had another flash of memory — her, age seven or eight, and her mother, just a child herself, around twenty-two or twenty-three. She stood a beautiful creature at a different mirror, a mirror with a jagged crack down the right-hand side, and performed this very action. She'd then turned swiftly and peered down at little Janine to say, "I won't be gone late." It was implicit back then that Nancy couldn't afford a babysitter. Janine wasn't invited out on her dates with men— men who would inevitably go on to treat her mother terribly.

Janine often didn't learn the full details of whatever had gone wrong with each. She only heard the screaming and crying, then watched as her mother fell into a dark pit and wrapped herself up in blankets and drank herself into a stupor.

Nancy turned now to find Janine stationed near her, wordless and overly quiet. Nancy jumped slightly, then forced a smile.

"Oh, darling, I didn't see you there," she said.

"You look nice," Janine returned. "That lipstick suits you perfectly."

Nancy glanced again toward the mirror and arched an eyebrow. "Do you think so? Elsa helped me pick it out the other day. I realized a few years ago that I couldn't get away with all that bright red lipstick any longer. Oh, but you were probably never such a red lipstick wearer, were you?"

Janine's voice quivered with her answer. "Jack's family wasn't so keen on bright red. I wore it exactly once, and I felt like Julia Roberts in *Pretty Woman*."

Nancy's lips parted with shock. After a dramatic pause, she burst into laughter, then dropped into the little hallway chair. "I have a feeling you have quite a few stories like that."

"Not many in recent memory," Janine offered. "Although those first few years..."

"The Potters aren't exactly known for their kindness," Nancy returned. "Every person in America knows that."

"And there I was. Smack-dab in the middle of them."

"And you even carry their last name."

They held the silence for a moment. Janine was surprised she'd been so candid with her mother as she had set out to be the exact opposite over the previous week. She thought about telling her mother that she'd just met some of the Katama Lodge's favorite local regulars, but she didn't want to toss Carmella into the flames before a proper introduction.

"What are you getting ready for?" Janine finally asked.

"Oh, it's silly, really." Nancy popped back up from the hallway chair to finalize her makeup. "There's a festival over in Oak Bluffs, and they want to honor Neal. I said I'd go and make some kind of speech. I don't know. I'm not really one for the spotlight."

There was the creak of a floorboard. Suddenly, off to the right, Elsa appeared on the steps. She wore a beautiful light butter yellow dress, which hugged her curves beautifully, and golden earrings dangled from her lobes. She gave Janine a tentative smile, then said, "Oh, I hope Nancy told you about the festival tonight? You really must join us."

"She won't want to go to some silly island festival," Nancy returned.

Janine turned her attention back to her mother. She wasn't entirely sure how to read Nancy's tone. Did she not want her daughter to attend? Or did she just not think Janine would want to waste her time doing such a thing?

"But it really is something special," Elsa said as she continued down the steps and joined her stepmother at the mirror. "You never got to meet Dad, but I know you would have loved him. Everyone did."

Janine caught her mother's eye. Nancy tilted her head as her irises glowed.

"I can stop by for a bit, sure," Janine said suddenly. "Just let me go change clothes."

Janine hustled up to her bedroom. Her decision to go to the festival both pleased her and annoyed her, all at once. On the one hand, what did she care about her mother giving a speech? And this island, with its festivals.

This was exactly the type of thing she was trying to avoid —attention of any kind. But on the other hand, her afternoon at the Katama Lodge had piqued her curiosity all the more. It was clear that Nancy Grimson Remington wasn't the woman Janine had grown up with any longer.

It was up to her to really see this woman for who she was.

* * *

The festival lined the Oak Bluffs Harbor. Near the line of sailboats, a large stage had been set up, and as they approached, a local band played a classic rock song, which had several festival revelers tapping their feet and singing along. Booth after booth offered fatty, greasy, absolutely delicious foods, and lights were strung from building to building to stall, giving the entire festival a feeling of magic and union.

Janine, Elsa, and Nancy walked through the crowd slowly, as many people reached a hand out to speak to Nancy, congratulating her on the award and offering their condolences for Neal.

"He was such a good man," one woman said as she shook her head.

"He changed my life," Nancy agreed. "As did this island. As did all of you."

When she said this, her eyes found Janine's again. It felt like a loaded statement.

"I'm sure you changed him just as much as he changed you," the woman said knowingly. "Neal had a hard road before you. Thank God he met you when he did."

At this, Elsa's face shifted strangely. Janine again felt a number of secrets beneath the surface.

"We sure do miss him," Nancy offered as her voice wavered.

Janine, Elsa, and Nancy gathered around a nearby local wine stall, where Elsa ordered them three glasses of chardonnay. This left Nancy and Janine at the stand-up table alone. Janine shifted her weight and watched as her mother scanned the festival-goers, seemingly nervous.

"Did you write your speech already?" Janine asked. She couldn't bear the silence a moment longer.

"What? Oh. Yes. I scribbled something down." Nancy seemed distracted. "Gosh, it's strange to be here without Neal. Every year, without fail, we shared a fried elephant ear and drank and laughed all night. He grew up on this island, and you could feel his love for it in everything he did. His love was always larger than life."

Janine watched as a young girl collected an elephant ear from the nearby booth. "We could share one if you want to?" She almost called her mother "Mom" there but held it back.

"Oh, I'm sure you wouldn't want that. You've spent the past twenty years eating caviar, haven't you?"

Janine spoke softly. "I'm still the girl who grew up on hot dogs and macaroni and cheese in Brooklyn."

Nancy's lips fell from her already strained smile. Luckily, Elsa returned with their glasses of wine, and Nancy and Janine were allowed to pretend they hadn't looked too long at their strange past. Elsa described the history of the little wine store to Janine, who pretended to take an interest, even as the information ran in one ear and out the other.

When a natural pause entered the conversation,

Janine heard herself ask, "Does your sister ever come to events like this?"

Elsa's chin dropped. "No. She doesn't have children or a partner or anything, and she tends to think events like this are kind of a waste of time."

Again, there it was: *that darkness between them.*

"Which reminds me. You really should meet my children and my grandbaby!" Elsa said. "I think Mallory is around here with baby Zachery somewhere."

Nancy announced she had to go get set up, as her speech was to be after the band finished. Janine followed Elsa through the bustling crowd, anxious for her mother's speech and feeling unfamiliar and not really fitting in. Kids who walked past her looked delirious from their sugar rushes; their lips were bright blue from cotton candy. Their parents' faces were glazed over from their drinks and tanned from the sun. You could feel expectation for the next summer months on everyone's lips.

In another reality, perhaps Janine would have allowed herself to feel happy, too.

And maybe, in a sense, she did feel it somewhere beneath the surface of her dark and chaotic soul.

Maybe she would even have some cotton candy later.

It wasn't like anybody was around to stop her. It wasn't like Jack's family would ogle her and ask her if she thought she should really do that. Even Maxine, who was always on one diet or another, wasn't around to scoff.

Elsa turned and beckoned for Janine to come closer. A beautiful girl, who was the spitting image of Elsa, but younger, stood holding a baby around one year old.

"Mallory, I'd like you to meet my stepsister, Janine." Elsa beamed as Janine stepped closer.

"Wow. Hello!" Mallory said. "I'm Mallory, and this is baby Zachery."

"Lovely to meet you." Janine willed her voice to sound more genuine, but she still felt awkward and strange.

"My fiancé is around here somewhere," Mallory continued. "I know he'd love to meet you, too, but he has a whole vendetta with one of the festival games. He wants to win baby Zachery a teddy bear, and I can't stop him."

"Sometimes, men get these ideas in their heads," Janine offered with a knowing smile.

Mallory laughed with a little snort. "Well said. Right now, it's like I have two kids at this festival instead of one."

At that moment, the band eased out of its last song. The lead singer remained at the microphone. He slipped his fingers through his black strands of hair and said, "May I have everyone's attention? We have a very important ceremony after this that you're going to want to hear."

Janine's throat constricted. She gulped back a bit of her wine and turned her eyes toward Elsa, suddenly nervous. In a few moments, the bandleader introduced Nancy Grimson Remington to the stage. She walked on thin legs, totally anxious, then gripped the microphone and tilted it down, making the speakers screech.

"Good evening, everyone," Nancy began.

Janine wished she could have stepped back in time to describe this scene to the teenage version of herself. *One day, your mother will be someone special. Someone loved. Someone revered.*

"I guess you all know who I am," Nancy continued with a nervous laugh, one that caused the rest of the festival-goers to chuckle, too. "But I'm not here for me, and you know that too. We all lost a great man about six months ago. My husband, and the love of my life, Neal Remington, passed on from this world and into the next. He left behind a pretty massive shadow."

"God bless Neal!" someone called from the audience as several others clapped.

Nancy's eyes glowed with tears.

"Over the years, Neal's Katama Lodge and Wellness Spa helped heal thousands of women from all over the world," Nancy continued. "We took in women from all walks of life, even when they couldn't fully pay for it. Neal was dedicated to his service. Sometimes, when I worried about whether we were giving too much away or letting people take advantage of us, he just said, 'Nancy? Listen to me. We have more than enough, and it's up to us to share it.'"

At this point, Nancy's voice broke, and she bent her head forward with sorrow. "I wish he was here with us today. He always knew what to say, and best of all, he knew when to stay quiet to let us feel what we needed to feel. I've been given this award for the Katama Lodge and Wellness Spa for continued service to the island of Martha's Vineyard. Thank you for honoring Neal and his life's work. Thank you."

Janine placed her glass of wine on a nearby table to smack her palms together as loudly as she could. She felt she'd never heard her mother be so sincere, so urgent, so beautifully poetic.

This woman—how was she possibly Nancy Grimson?

Nancy left the stage after that to allow another band

to set up. Elsa whispered in Janine's ear, "She's always such a class act, isn't she?"

Janine suddenly felt she couldn't breathe properly. She excused herself from the crowd and hustled off to the side, where she could inhale and exhale deeply in the direction of the water. Everything in her life felt like a strange and spinning storm. She wasn't sure when she would feel calm again.

Just then, she spotted a man with a video camera located off to the side of the stage. He had dark curls, and his dark eyebrows were furrowed low over his eyes.

It was Henry, the documentarian.

Janine hadn't seen him since they'd watched his camera get swallowed whole by the ocean.

Janine maneuvered around the backs of the various food stalls and wound her way toward Henry. When she reached him, she waited for him to take his camera down, then she took a deep breath and tapped him on the shoulder. He turned toward her slowly. When he realized who she was, he reacted only slightly. There was no malice to his face but no joy, either.

"Hey," Janine finally said.

"Hello there." He arched an eyebrow, then said, "No bike accident or camera destruction yet. What do you have up your sleeve this time?"

Janine laughed slightly. "I really want to apologize to you. You're this — strange person from my past, and I have not been very kind."

Henry gave a half shrug. "I think I can understand that. According to the magazines, you've been through hell. Not that I read the magazines."

"Right." Janine's heart fluttered slightly. "Anyway. I would really love to repay you in any way possible."

Henry waved his hand. "The camera was insured. Not a problem at all. I only hope my other one is getting used down under, you know?"

"As we speak, a mermaid is filming a whale somewhere off the coast of North Carolina," Janine offered with a laugh.

"Wow, I would kill for that footage," Henry returned.

They studied one another for a moment. Janine's throat tightened again.

"I'm sorry about what you said. About my husband leaving your last project on the cutting room floor," Janine told him.

"It happens in this business. I'm used to it. I shouldn't have said anything. This was years ago."

"I guess there was a reason I hadn't heard of you for a while," Janine said.

Silence fell between them. Janine felt strangely hollow.

Finally, she asked, "What are you working on now? You don't have to tell me. I've just seen you around with your camera, and well, I'm curious. You're obviously a city guy with an interest in Martha's Vineyard."

"Ah." Henry looked doubtful for a moment. "You really want to know?"

"Yes. Of course, I do." Janine tilted her head slightly and then added, "I would love to know how you see this place. I've been so shell-shocked since I got here that I'm not sure if I see it correctly."

Henry nodded. "Okay. Okay, I'll show you." He flipped his phone out of his pocket with a flourish. His hands were large, sure of themselves. He typed her number into his phone evenly, then said, "I'll be in touch."

When Janine walked away, her heart thudded in her throat. It was the first time she'd given her number to a man in twenty-four years. It thrilled her and terrified her. It made her feel outside of herself, though — and wasn't that the goal?

Chapter Fourteen

"You sound different, Mom." Maggie's voice was a comfort against the shell of Janine's ear as she cuddled herself into a ball in bed later that night. "Are you okay?"

Janine had just described the Oak Bluffs festival, along with Nancy's speech, to her daughter. She'd had two glasses of wine with very little dinner and felt a bit foggy and far away. In truth, she missed Maggie and Alyssa desperately; she missed her thousand-count sheets and her favorite Italian restaurant and her routine runs in Central Park. Beyond everything, though, she missed Maxine, her best friend, her other half.

"I'm okay, honey," Janine whispered. "Just a bit sad, is all."

"But Grandma sounds really extraordinary," Maggie said brightly. "She sounds like a completely different woman than the one you always described to us."

"I think she's going through something," Janine said softly.

"You both lost quite a lot this year."

"I just don't know if we have it in us to hold one another up," Janine confessed sadly. "Maybe too much has happened."

Maggie spoke a bit about the wedding dresses she'd seen recently during a perusal with Alyssa at a very expensive boutique in Manhattan. Janine's heart twitched with sadness. Wedding dress shopping? She was supposed to be there.

"But don't worry. We won't pick anything out until you're here," Maggie assured her, as though she could sense her mother's sadness. "You have the best taste out of all of us, anyway. I wouldn't trust myself."

Janine remembered the outfit she'd worn for the festival that night: a sundress borrowed from Elsa, and nothing she would have ever picked for herself, given the status of her position as Jack's wife.

Did this mean that one day soon, she would wear red lipstick and not even deem it a little bit rash?

"Have you thought any more about what you'll do next?" Maggie asked after a strange pause.

Janine glanced at the desk, on which the list she'd begun to draw up sat expectantly. She sat upright and then pressed her hand against her forehead. "I've been thinking again about my practice, naturopathic medicine."

"Mom! Wow. That's fantastic. That was your heart and soul. Alyssa and I could never figure out exactly why you just closed shop and quit."

Janine's stomach jumped with guilt. Had she really quit in some attempt to take better control over her life with Jack? How pathetic. How strange.

"Nancy's Katama Lodge and Wellness Spa has been closed since her husband's death," Janine said softly.

"And I think they could use someone like me. I just — I don't want to get ahead of myself. And I don't even know if Nancy would be up for something like that, you know? We certainly didn't get along back in the old days. I don't know what it would mean to work together."

"If she wasn't up for it, you could always come back to the city and build your practice here again," Maggie informed her. "You have all of your old patients, and I'm sure they wouldn't even hesitate to return to you if they found out you opened up again."

Again, Janine felt the massive shadow of Jack Potter with Maxine alongside him. It was as though they now ruled Manhattan. Janine was only their tossed-away garbage.

"Maybe," Janine said. "I still think it's too soon. I'll cross that bridge when I get to it."

* * *

The following day, around noon, Janine walked again toward the Katama Lodge and Wellness Spa. When she entered the foyer, she found Carmella behind the desk with a phone latched to her ear as she took furious notes.

"Yes. We do have an opening next week on Thursday, but not until after two. Would you rather switch to Friday? Okay, perfect. Yes. See you then."

Carmella lifted a finger high as she set the date in the calendar. She then turned back toward Janine and delivered a bright smile.

"Hi! Welcome to Katama Lodge and Wellness Center." A little wrinkle formed between her brows. "I think I remember you in here yesterday, right?"

"That's right," Janine said as she pressed her hands against the cool wood of the antique desk.

"But I didn't have a chance to schedule you," Carmella said.

"I actually left in a hurry," Janine explained. "But those women, your regulars, they really made me understand what this place was like in its glory days."

Carmella's eyes fluttered around the room as though she was cast into a sea of memories. "It certainly was a wonderful haven for so many," she whispered. "I'm glad that we can offer at least a little bit of that after all that's happened."

Janine's heart thudded with apprehension. "I actually wanted to talk to you about that."

Carmella arched an eyebrow. "I'm sorry?"

"I haven't been totally truthful. My name is Janine Potter. I'm— well, your stepsister."

Carmella's lips parted slowly as realization sparkled in her eyes. "I see. You're Nancy's daughter. Manhattan, right? Upper West Side?"

"More money than God in a previous life. Yes. That was me," Janine offered.

Carmella heaved a sigh. "You should have told me who you were yesterday."

"You were busy. I didn't want to bother you."

"I guess you probably told your mom that I've reopened the acupuncture studio? Elsa wasn't so happy about it, and I don't think Nancy would be either if she knows about it," Carmella continued.

"I haven't told her anything. My mother and I, well. We aren't exactly good at telling each other things."

Carmella's eyes grew shadowed. "I see." She rolled her shoulders back. "I have to say, that surprises me.

Nancy was always so open with Elsa at least. They're two peas in a pod."

"I've noticed that," Janine offered. "It's just as weird for me as it is for you, I bet."

Carmella glanced down at her calendar. "I don't have another appointment for fifteen minutes. I could sit with you for a bit. Do you want a tea?"

"No. I'll be fine."

Janine and Carmella sat on the two overly cloud-like cozy chairs to the right of the receptionist's desk. They held the silence for a few seconds until Janine said, "I don't know what you know about my previous life, but you should know it's over. I don't have much of anything right now. But it seems to me that my mother doesn't, either."

The wrinkle between Carmella's eyebrows deepened.

"I've been trained in naturopathic medicine," Janine continued. "I practiced for over a decade but then discontinued my practice. It's one of my biggest regrets."

"I had no idea. Did you know your mother worked here?"

"No idea," Janine echoed.

"How strange that you were both drawn to the same type of work in health," Carmella said.

"It's especially strange if you knew more about our past," Janine murmured. "Although maybe there's something to be said about us both craving the idea of being healed."

"Nancy never speaks about her time in New York," Carmella commented. "Maybe Elsa knows more than I do. I'm sure Dad did, although he thought the world of

Nancy. He would have never rubbed her nose in it. Whatever it was."

There was a mirror on the far end of the receptionist hall. Janine caught her own reflection and thought again how strangely she was dressed. Her Manhattan clothes just didn't fly here. She wore slacks, a little T-shirt that highlighted her thin arms, and a pair of tennis shoes, which were comfortable for the longer walks she'd begun to take. Walks that had nothing to do with the frantic nature of the city and everything to do with the sweeping waves and the twittering birds and the glorious sky above.

"Neal sounds like a remarkable man," Janine said.

"He was. But also, we had our problems. Quite a number of problems, in fact," Carmella continued. "Maybe you've already noticed that my sister and I don't exactly cling to each other. We haven't spoken all week. I talk more with her daughter, Mallory, than I do with Elsa."

"Family problems. I know them well."

Carmella exhaled slowly. "So you're suggesting that in some way, you want to help reopen this place?"

"Yes, that's exactly what I'm proposing," Janine said, her voice laced with assurance. She felt as though this new endeavor was her calling.

"That's what I want, too," Carmella confided. "I miss it so much. Even back then, because Elsa and Nancy and I all had a common goal, we got along a whole lot better. Dad was in the mix, too. It just felt like we all belonged together, despite our little arguments. Now, we don't have the central heartbeat of our family, which is this lodge. I have to do the acupuncture stuff to keep my head above water, but..."

"But if we opened it up, it could maybe heal all of us."

"Not just the women who seek us out," Carmella whispered.

"It could be difficult to get Nancy to agree to it," Janine said after a pause.

Carmella arched an eyebrow again at the first-name use. "Nancy. Huh. Yeah, you guys aren't close, are you?"

Janine shrugged. "Maybe we could be. I don't know. I don't know if our relationship is a house that needs fixing or if the house has already burned down."

"Well, I think my father would say something here like: you can always rebuild," Carmella returned with a smile.

"I should say the same to you, maybe," Janine said.

"Not so simple," Carmella offered.

"Mine, neither."

"Right. Well. Okay." Carmella slapped her palms together as her upcoming client entered the foyer. "Let's meet to discuss this with Nancy and Elsa. Ease them into it. Maybe you could outline all your plans and what your role would be."

"Okay. Okay." Janine's heart swelled with excitement.

Carmella's eyes turned over the foyer again as she clucked her tongue. "I would love to have this place bustling again."

"Maybe we can make it happen. Maybe it's not too late."

Chapter Fifteen

Henry's text message arrived on another beautiful morning that Tuesday after the Oak Bluffs festival. Janine was on a jog, and when she glanced at her phone to switch the music, she spotted an unknown number along with a message:

> UNKNOWN: Hello. Would you like to meet me at the Edgartown Lighthouse this afternoon around three?

> UNKNOWN: It's Henry, by the way.

> UNKNOWN: (The man whose life you've been trying to ruin.)

She stopped short on her jogging path in total shock. Her stomach immediately cramped, and she held onto her side. Her nose scrunched as she tried to focus on her breathing. Even though she was in pretty good shape, she wasn't twenty-five anymore. It was sometimes difficult for her to remember that.

As though God himself wanted to remind her of this,

a twentysomething male runner whipped past her just then, his tanned skin glistening with sweat and sunlight.

"All right," Janine said. "I get it."

She stepped to the side and sat at the edge of a rock, her hands cupping her phone. In the distance, children scampered through the waves and splashed one another while their mothers sat nearby on a picnic blanket. Janine remembered those long-ago days when she'd had the girls at the park, and she'd had conversations with other young mothers, all of whom had grown up in Manhattan and knew her to be young, just starting out, and the one who'd married Jack Potter somehow.

Janine took a deep breath and then reread Henry's texts.

Finally, she responded.

> JANINE: Hey! I promise—no more life-ruining. Three sounds good. See you there.

She scrunched her nose at the response. It seemed flat, with no emotion, and not very personable. Then again, she had no idea who this guy was, really. She respected him as an artist and resented that he'd once been kind of chummy with Jack. Still, her curiosity surrounding him was heavy, something she couldn't ignore, like that itch that just won't go away.

Janine wore a light yellow dress, one she had borrowed from Elsa, and slipped a cardigan in her purse, just in case the weather shifted. It was seventy-five degrees, an actual perfect day, and as she stepped out from Nancy's house, the sea breeze fluttered through her dark hair beautifully.

Elsa stood out near her car and waved a hand. She'd

agreed to drive Janine over to the Edgartown Lighthouse, as it wasn't exactly in walking distance. When Janine thanked her again, Elsa just said, "Don't mention it. I have a few errands I want to run in town, and then I told Mallory I would babysit Zachery."

"That's kind of you," Janine said.

"You know, I love that little boy," Elsa said as she slipped into the front seat and buckled up. "It was a hard time when he was born. My husband died exactly one week after."

"That's awful."

"He got to hold him, though. Before he passed away," Elsa offered. "It was a blessing."

Janine marveled at the sort of woman Elsa was: so good, so wholesome that she considered her husband's status as one of the living for only a week after their grandson's birth to be a "blessing." Janine wished she could see things in such a light of positivity.

Maybe she could learn from her.

"Who did you say you were meeting?" Elsa asked as they snaked through the country roads, northeast, toward the lighthouse.

"I ran into an old friend," Janine began. "I knew him in Manhattan. I had no idea he'd be on the island."

"Wow. Funny where life takes us, isn't it?"

Janine wanted to say, *you have no idea*, but she kept the sentiment to herself. She didn't want to point too specifically at how strange the next hour or so was about to be. She was already nervous enough as it was.

* * *

Henry was already at the lighthouse. Janine watched him from the sidewalk as he took a number of shots, holding the camera steady as he stepped leftward, trying to circle the old building. After five minutes, Janine stepped toward him, and he whipped the camera around to film her instead. She blushed and waved her hands.

"I told you. No paparazzi," she teased.

He chuckled and dropped the camera to his side. His dark locks were every which way, and they snuck around his ears and toward the nape of his neck. His eyes glowed with good humor, and he'd developed even more of a tan than before. Janine wondered what he'd been up to. Hiking. Swimming. Boating.

She supposed she had something of a tan, too.

"Hey there," he said. "I'm glad you came."

Janine blushed at how upfront he was. She glanced toward the lighthouse, which was enormous and white, with a wraparound railing at the top beneath the black pillar.

"I've always thought lighthouses were really romantic," she said as she stepped closer to him. "Something about the idea of living in them and keeping the light going and ensuring sailors could get home. It's all so dramatic."

"It really is," Henry agreed. "But this one, in particular, holds a lot of sentiment for me."

"Why's that?"

Henry heaved a sigh. "Well, this lighthouse. It used to have a family in it years and years and years ago, and the head of that family was my great-great-grandfather."

"No!"

"Yes." A slight smile hovered at the edge of his lips.

"Wow." Janine studied his face contemplatively, no

longer interested in the lighthouse. She tried to imagine a rugged-looking man, artistic and powerful, like Henry, operating the lighthouse, day in and day out and all through the night. "So you're from the island."

"Yes, I am. A true islander, I suppose," Henry said. "But come on. Let's go in. I want to get some shots from the interior."

Janine followed Henry up toward the lighthouse, which now operated as a museum. Henry had apparently cleared it with the council to get two passes that allowed them up a steep ladder straight to the top. Henry allowed Janine to go up ahead of him, and Janine grabbed each rung gingerly, terrified she would make one wrong move and fall below. Beyond that, of course, she wore a simple little yellow dress that she now regretted, and she prayed that Henry wouldn't lift his chin to catch sight of her satin panties. How embarrassing.

But once they arrived at the top, Henry set up his camera to take a beautiful shot of the Bay just beyond the lighthouse. The air inside the windmill itself was stuffy, and it reeked of moldy old wood.

"This old lighthouse isn't the official lighthouse, though," Henry explained as he continued to take his shot. "The original was built in 1828. It was built due to the whaling boom of the late 1700s and early 1800s."

"Whaling boom. Wow," Janine breathed. "I'm such a city girl. Everything you're saying is foreign to my ears."

Henry chuckled. "I understand perfectly well. Back then, the lighthouse keeper—"

"Someone you're related to, I guess?"

"I think so. I think it was passed down, father to son, until it closed. But the keeper lived a distance from the lighthouse and had to row to the lighthouse. Very soon after, they built a wooden causeway. And here's the saddest part."

"Oh no."

"The causeway was known around here as the Bridge of Sighs," he continued. "Because the wives and daughters of the whalers would come out and stand on the causeway to watch them depart. Sometimes, their voyages would last up to five years."

Janine gazed out across the waters with her heart in her throat. Five years was an incredible amount of time. She couldn't imagine it — having such enormous love for someone who headed out on an adventure without assurance of their return.

"Why did your great-great-grandfather leave the lighthouse?"

"It was destroyed," Henry said with a sad smile. "The Hurricane of 1938 was a real doozy, apparently. They brought the lighthouse we're currently standing in from Ipswich."

"Huh. I wonder what Ipswich feels about Edgartown stealing their history."

"At least it's something pretty to look at," Henry said with an ironic laugh. "And my documentary about my family and the history of the island wouldn't look right without several lighthouse shots."

"So that's your documentary," Janine said.

Henry removed his camera from his eyes and gave a light shrug. "It's difficult to explain, maybe. If I had to write up a synopsis for the purpose of funding, I might not be able to put it into words."

Just then, one of the workers down below hollered that they'd run out of time. Slowly, Henry and Janine stepped down the ladder. When Janine's feet found solid ground again, she breathed a sigh of relief. Yet again, she was reminded of just how not-twenty-five she was.

Back outside, they began to wander down the board-walk, back toward the center of Edgartown. Janine had hardly explored the little town, as she'd generally kept to the southern part of the island. When she looked at her time on Martha's Vineyard, it was difficult to comprehend that nearly two weeks had passed since her departure from New York. She'd begun to let go of bits and pieces of her anger without realizing it. When she looked at her heart, it still ached with sadness — but it was no longer as black.

It was almost too easy to walk alongside Henry. Janine had the strangest sensation that he understood when she needed to be quiet, as though their souls spoke to one another beneath the surface of verbal under-standing.

Probably, that was all in her head, though.

After a long, comfortable silence, Janine said, "I would really love to hear more about your documentary."

"Of course." Henry stopped short at the end of the dock and turned out again toward the water so that a sea breeze fluttered through his thick, black curls. "I grew up on this island— specifically Edgartown. And I always knew this held such an amazing history, that my great-great-grandfather was the lighthouse keeper, and that my family went through a bit of turmoil during the twentieth century. There was some illness, some death, and some accidents. Run of the mill, maybe, but you can feel the cracks in our history. You can still feel the sadness that accompanies all those stories."

Janine felt she understood that, too. She still felt the rifts within her and her mother's relationship, twenty-five years after the fact. Probably, there were echoes of Nancy's relationship with her own mother, who had died when she'd been fourteen — something that had probably led to her pregnancy at the young age of sixteen.

"Sometimes, I think we're slaves to our past," Janine whispered.

Henry nodded. "I think that, sometimes, too. But this is why I want to make this documentary. I want to own the past in a way and understand my family and this island better. I want to know why I wanted so badly to leave this place. On paper, it's so perfect, isn't it?"

"And in real life, too," Janine added.

"I just can't help but feel that so far, what I've made is pretty flat," Henry said. "My mother just died. And I thought that would kick-start all these feelings around the island. But instead, I just have a lot of long shots of boats and that lighthouse and the occasional festival. I don't know. Maybe it's impossible to really see something that's so much a part of you."

Janine thought for a long moment. She considered what she'd seen in her two weeks on the island — the community she had witnessed at Katama Lodge and Wellness Spa and the festival along the Oak Bluffs Harbor. Already, it seemed she'd heard so many stories and witnessed so many ways in which the people of Martha's Vineyard held one another's stories close and helped them through their personal pain or illness.

"Out of curiosity, why haven't you interviewed people on the island yet?" Janine asked. "I mean, if you want to get a full picture of the place, that is."

Henry tilted his head. "I have considered it. But to me, these people are just the people I grew up alongside. I don't really know what to ask them because I feel like I already know what's in their heads."

Janine smiled. "I think everyone can surprise you. Especially the ones you think won't."

Suddenly, with some kind of power she'd never known she had, Janine grabbed Henry's elbow and led him toward a bench, which overlooked the water. There, she found an older gentleman who gazed contemplatively out across the Bay.

"Excuse me, sir," Janine said brightly. "This is Henry. My name is Janine. And we're making a documentary about the history of the island."

The man gave no sign of being afraid or annoyed. In fact, his ears perked up slightly. "You don't say."

"We were curious if we could ask you a few questions," Janine said. "Only if you're comfortable."

The man agreed. Henry gave a slight shrug and then set up his camera from behind the bench so that the man turned around the bench to gaze into the camera, with a view of the sailboats in front of him. Even Janine had to admit that it was a perfect shot.

"Maybe first, you could introduce yourself?" Janine said as Henry pressed play.

"Sure," the man said. "My name is Stan Ellis."

"Stan, hello," Janine said. "Were you born on the island?"

"I wasn't, no," Stan replied. "Came here in my thirties and was completely blown away by it all. It's a unique place."

"We're similar, I guess," Janine said. "I just arrived here for the first time, age forty-three."

"Then you must feel it," Stan said. He gripped the top of the bench with bright white fingers. "There's a magic in the air here. And the people you meet genuinely care about everyone else's well-being. I've had a hard road of it — a damn strange path. But right now, just because of this island and the way the islanders know how to forgive, I'm in the happiest mental state of my life. I have a stepson who recently decided to move to the island. He keeps me busy and makes sure I go to all my doctor's appointments. If you had told me a year ago that anybody would ever demand I go to the doctor to keep in good health, I would have told you that you're a damn liar."

Stan chuckled as Janine's heart swelled. She glanced back toward Henry, whose eyes were enormous. It was really like they'd struck gold with this man. Before, he'd just been a stranger sitting on a bench. Now, they were collecting his story.

And the afternoon continued on in a similar fashion. Janine and Henry approached a number of walkers and restaurant owners and service staff members and innkeepers, and they asked them what they loved most about the island and if they wanted to share any stories. When they entered the Frosted Delights bakery, Jennifer, the redheaded owner whom Janine had met previously, told a sorrowful tale about her twin sister, who had drowned at age seventeen.

"Since then, I've done my best to think of her as much throughout the day as I can," Jennifer said somberly. "She's in the air, the water, the sun, and the sky. She's rooted within this island and will be forever. And I can feel her love everywhere."

At seven thirty, Henry and Janine grabbed ice cream cones and headed back out to the boardwalk. Janine couldn't remember the last time she had allowed herself to give in to the allure of a strawberry ice cream cone, and she reveled in it, even as it dripped down the sides and onto her fingers.

"That was quite a day, Janine," Henry finally said.

"I could have listened to people telling their stories for the next several hours, I think."

"I don't even know if I can use all of them for the documentary, but it definitely gave me a better understanding of this place," Henry continued. "It's not very creative of me to think that everyone around here is boring."

Janine grinned. "Well. Not everyone can be as exciting as you."

Henry scoffed. "I don't know about that. I used to think that about myself. But right now, I'm just here in the place I grew up. And I don't even know if I want to go back to the city, really. I'm forty-five years old, and I feel rootless."

"That makes two of us. I'm pretty rootless, too," Janine admitted. "And sometimes it fills me with shame late at night."

"What do you feel in the morning?"

Janine gave a light shrug. "I try to tell myself that everything happens for a reason. But I don't even know if that's true."

Henry held her gaze for a long time, so long that she felt another droplet of pink ice cream across her knuckles.

"I have to believe that's true," he finally admitted. "It's the reason we tell stories. It's the reason I make documentaries. We have to make sense of our past and how it brought us here. It's all purposeful. It really is."

"I hope you're right," Janine whispered. "I hope all that pain was for a reason."

Chapter Sixteen

Carmella picked Janine up at the house the following afternoon at three thirty. When Janine slipped into her car, she entered a Carmella world of Alanis Morisette CDs and a very powerful perfume and a pile of clothing in the back seat, which Carmella explained was there "just in case" something came up.

"I was always sort of a live wire," she said as she eased out of the driveway and backed out onto the main road. "Dad wasn't sure what to do with me as a teenager."

Janine laughed good-naturedly. "And your mother? What about her?"

Carmella shifted strangely. "Elsa and Nancy really haven't told you much of anything, have they?"

Janine's heart fluttered with fear. "I guess not."

"Suffice it to say, Mom died when I was pretty young. And it wasn't the first loss in our little nuclear family," Carmella said as she flipped her dark hair behind her shoulder. "Loss has been a part of this family's policy since the very beginning. I guess it's part of the reason Elsa and I can barely look at each other any longer."

Janine wasn't sure what to say. She felt she'd "stepped in it." She folded and unfolded her hands on her lap and blinked out the window. In the distance, she spotted someone riding on horseback, and she wondered if it was her mother.

"So have you told Nancy about our little dinner party tonight?" Carmella asked.

"I mentioned that I wanted to cook since Elsa will be away tonight. She said it was no trouble. That we could just order food in or something," Janine said. "But I insisted."

"I see." Carmella adjusted her hands across the steering wheel. She'd painted her nails a dark burgundy and they glowed with afternoon light.

"I'm a bit nervous, to be honest," Janine continued. "Nancy has seemed really down since the festival in Oak Bluffs. I haven't seen much of her."

"Strange," Carmella said.

"I'm worried that my coming here has put her in an even worse position. I mean, maybe she thought we would see each other and have this big loving reunion. But we're both fresh off heartaches. It's like because we're both damaged that were not strong enough to fix all the stuff that happened before I married Jack."

Carmella heaved a sigh. "Well, I still think we should try to convince her to reopen. Maybe it could be the first step toward something good, a healing opportunity for so many, including yourselves. I don't know."

"I don't know, either."

Janine and Carmella walked somberly through the aisles of the local Edgartown grocery store. Several people greeted Carmella brightly, and she hardly offered them a smile in return. This was such a contrast to Elsa, who normally stayed at the grocery store for a full hour due to the number of people they ran into. In the past weeks, this had annoyed Janine, who'd always had to stand nearby, shifting her weight, prepared to wave a hand in hello when she was introduced as Nancy's "real" daughter. "How fun for you! A new sister!" one woman had said to Elsa as though they were ten years old and not forty.

But now, it struck Janine as strange, the difference between Elsa and Carmella. It also struck her how terribly sad it was.

Back at the house, Janine watched as Carmella marched through the kitchen with authority. After all, she had been raised there and knew where everything was stored. Probably, she had a million memories between those walls — certainly some dark ones, too.

They prepared salmon, potatoes, and homemade rolls, along with a lemon cake for dessert. As they cooked, Janine poured them both glasses of merlot, and they clinked and said, "Good luck to us."

Around seven thirty, Janine poured her mother a glass of wine. Still, there was no sound of her from the upstairs hallway. Janine's and Carmella's eyes turned upward in expectation.

"Maybe she's taking a nap?" Janine offered.

"She was never one for naps back in the old days," Carmella said. "She was always go-go-go. I never understood where she got all her energy."

Janine shivered, remembering that back in her time with Nancy, the woman had needed copious naps. She'd sometimes slept all through the day and night.

"Maybe I'll just go check on her," Janine said. "Just in case."

Janine made her way up the stairs and found herself in front of a closed door. She was reminded again of having to wake her mother years before when she'd needed someone to take her to school. She had been only seven and still a bit frightened to walk the streets alone. It had taken her maybe ten minutes to wake her mother, who'd reeked of alcohol at the time.

The Nancy Grimson Remington, who appeared on the other side of the door now, though, smelled of vanilla. She blinked tired eyes out from the darkness and yawned as she asked, "Is it already time for dinner?"

"It is," Janine said. She tried to keep her voice bright.

Nancy placed a hand over her eye as she exhaled. "I just don't know if I can make it, Janine. I'm terribly exhausted all the time."

Depression. Here it was again, knocking angrily at Nancy Grimson's door.

"There's no rush," Janine tried. "You can wear your pajamas if you want to. But it would be good to eat something. Don't you think?"

Nancy held Janine's gaze for a long while. It was obvious she wanted to get out of dinner.

"Just a few minutes. Just a few bites," Janine tried.

Nancy slipped her fingers through her hair. She seemed to weigh up possible options and ways she could get out of it. After another long pause, she said, "Oh, of course. I'll have some dinner. Sure." She sounded resigned.

There was such distance between them, mother and daughter. Janine felt Nancy's tentative footsteps behind her as they returned to the kitchen, then to the porch that over-looked the water. Carmella placed the last of the three plates on the table and then turned to smile at her stepmother.

Nancy stopped short in the doorway. "Carmella. What are you doing here?" Her eyes turned back toward Janine with confusion.

"We just want to talk to you about something." Carmella furrowed her brow.

Nancy looked on the verge of tumbling to her knees. She took a few steps forward, then collapsed at the table and blinked down at the pink fish, which was glossy with lemon juice. Janine and Carmella joined her at the table. Janine sipped her wine nervously, wondering if her mother would lift her head. Out there in the light, Nancy looked even more depressed than she had in the shadowy bedroom.

"Nancy, I don't know if Elsa has told you, but I started back up with my acupuncture appointments at the Lodge," Carmella began tentatively.

"She didn't, no," Nancy returned. She then swallowed and shifted her eyes toward Carmella. "And to be honest, that surprises me. I told you. I needed a break from the Lodge. Elsa does, too."

"I know that, Nancy," Carmella stammered. "But I need to keep my appointments going. And it's helped me to focus on something other than myself. To focus on the patients."

Nancy's cheek twitched. "I wish you would have told me this before you started."

"Elsa made it clear it wasn't wanted," Carmella said. "I didn't want to hurt you."

Nancy turned her eyes back toward Janine. Shadows

lurked beneath her eyes. "And what does this have to do with you, Janine?"

Janine's heart hammered. "I don't know if you know this, but I worked in naturopathic medicine for the previous decade or so. I'm a licensed naturopathic doctor, but I ended my practice about two years ago. I've really missed it ever since."

Nancy held Janine's eyes as shock made her lips part.

"What are the chances, Nancy? You and your daughter were drawn to the same practice, the same calling. To heal people," Carmella said.

Janine felt anxious now, her heart hammering in her chest. Her palms felt clammy. "I told Carmella I would be interested in helping you reopen if you wanted that. I would love to reinstate my practice."

"And she would be perfect for the Lodge, Nancy," Carmella continued. "Since we lost Carlos, and of course, Dad, we have big shoes to fill, but Janine can fill those shoes."

"We thought we could even do a soft opening around July 4," Janine continued. "We could have a party. Host some of the islanders who love the lodge the most. It's already clear that Martha's Vineyard misses the Katama Lodge. I met a few of Carmella's acupuncture clients, and they told me some absolutely amazing stories."

Nancy's eyes filled with tears as silence shrouded them. After a long pause, she murmured, "I'm sure it's difficult for you, Janine. You can't understand what we lost, with Neal gone."

"Of course," Janine tried hurriedly. "And I don't even want to pretend that I can understand. It's just—"

"But if we were to reopen, I would need Elsa. Elsa was Neal's right-hand woman," Nancy continued. "And

Carmella, you know better than anyone that Elsa needs this time off. She can hardly stand upright some days. She's lost so much."

Carmella's eyes flashed with a sense of knowing. "She won't talk to me."

Nancy dropped her chin. "I don't know what to say. This is your family, Carmella. This was your father's lodge before I ever entered the picture."

"But we need you. We need you to help us reopen it." Carmella's voice was low but urgent. "You've been a part of our family for over a decade now, Nancy. You—"

"It's not as though you cared for me much, Carmella." Nancy's voice was somber.

Carmella leaned back in her chair, almost in resignation. She looked physically injured; her face was scrunched. "We worked well together. You can't deny that."

"But maybe that chapter is closed, now." Nancy turned her eyes back toward the pink fish. "It's really up to Elsa. I won't move forward without her."

Carmella scoffed. "Here we go again. You and Elsa—the A team. Always working against me."

Nancy bristled. "We never worked against you, Carmella. You always searched for ways to think we were hurting you, against you, but it was never true."

Carmella seethed. After a dramatic pause, she shot up from her chair, sipped the last of her wine, and turned her eyes toward Janine. "I should have known this wouldn't work." She then stormed off the porch, letting the screen door slam after her.

Janine's shoulders slumped forward. She felt at a loss. Why had she thought they could convince her mother of anything, especially as she and Nancy had hardly begun to heal their own relationship? There was so much darkness within this family. So many unhealed wounds. They required years and years of therapy, maybe — that, or just the rest of their lives apart.

Nancy muttered as she stood from her untouched fish. "I'm sorry, Janine. I just don't know. I just don't know."

Janine stewed around in these final words as she stared out across the ocean waves. Three untouched plates of fish remained, even as she poured herself a second, then a third glass of wine. She marveled at the tiny thread of hope she had felt. She reasoned that soon, she would have to pack up and return to the city to deal with the gravity of her own despair and build her life anew. Maybe there was nothing here on the Vineyard for her, after all.

Chapter Seventeen

The following morning, around seven thirty, Janine called her daughter, Maggie. They hadn't spoken in several days, and Maggie's voice was bright and eager when she answered, as though she'd been worried. Janine hated this, the idea that her daughters needed to worry about her. She wanted to be the kind of woman who could stand on her own two feet.

"How did it go with pitching the reopening to Grandma?" Maggie asked after a few pleasantries.

"Not so well, Mags. She doesn't want to do it without Elsa, and Elsa and Carmella hardly even speak."

"That's really sad. I googled the place last night. Gwyneth Paltrow stayed there once and put it on her list of top-ten relaxing retreats on the East Coast."

"Gwyneth, huh? Well, she would know what she's talking about."

"It just stinks. It seems like a perfect way for everyone to come back together," Maggie said.

"I know. But maybe it's not meant to be," Janine returned. "Besides. I have you girls back in the city.

Maybe I can start my practice up again. Get a tiny apartment in Brooklyn, maybe even around the corner from where I used to live."

"Prices in Brooklyn aren't what they used to be," Maggie offered with a dry laugh.

"Sure. But they aren't comparable to high-rise apartments in the Upper West Side, either," Janine pointed out.

"Fair." Maggie paused for a moment. There was the sound of something being poured, maybe coffee. "Dad said he sent along the divorce papers already."

"I know. I have them here," Janine said, remembering how she'd shoved them in the very bottom of a desk drawer there at her mother's place. "Have you seen a lot of him?"

"No," Maggie insisted. "Hardly at all. And never with her."

Her. Maxine. A woman Maggie surely loved almost as much as she loved her own mother. How difficult it all was.

"I just don't know if I'll ever be able to forgive him," Maggie said softly. "You said it yourself. Sometimes, there are things you just can't get over. No matter how much time has passed."

* * *

Janine donned jogging shorts and a tank top and slid her feet into some tennis shoes. She made up her mind to peruse apartment options, potentially call Jack for some kind of loan, and set up a meeting with a lawyer who could help her figure out her options. After all, she had signed that prenup, but she'd also been his wife, the mother of his children, for twenty-four years. She was certain she'd be entitled to something.

She was glad she'd begun to think clearly, even if she still felt like a fish out of water.

When she reached the front porch, she found her mother seated there with a cup of coffee and a slab of toast, on which she'd smeared butter and a thin layer of strawberry jam. Nancy's hands were folded across the table dutifully, and her eyes seemed far away, as though she'd stepped from this dimension into the next.

"Mom?" Janine said the word evenly, then realized, with a strange jolt, that she hadn't called Nancy that in years. It sounded so strange coming from her lips.

Nancy turned her head slowly and blinked at her daughter, seemingly confused. "Hello, Janine. Are you off for a run?"

"I'd planned on it."

"You're looking quite trim. Strong." Nancy glanced at her uneaten toast and added, "I haven't had much energy lately. I should push myself like you are. You've lost just as much as I have."

Janine wasn't sure what to say. She found herself slipping into a chair beside Nancy and following her gaze. Sometimes, she thought, all you had to do to be there for someone was to sit with them. Sometimes, words just couldn't do what you needed them to.

"I've thought about it long and hard, and I think I want to sell the Katama Lodge," Nancy said finally. "I'll split the funds with my husband's girls. And then, maybe, I'll leave the island behind. I see Neal in everything. I feel him everywhere. And I just worry if I don't get away and try something new, I'll never be able to move forward."

Janine was suddenly reminded of the previous

version of Nancy: the one who hadn't been able to hold down a job for longer than two months; the one who'd forced them to move from apartment to apartment as a way to hide from landlords she owed money to. This woman before her, this was the one who wanted to run. This wasn't Neal's Nancy. This was Janine's Nancy.

"Nancy, these people on this island, they love you," Janine whispered. "I see it everywhere—the woman at the bakery and the people at the festival. Heck, your step-daughter, Elsa, thinks you're the sun and the moon and the stars put together."

Nancy stole a side glance at her daughter and then shrugged. Little hollows formed in her cheeks as she said, "I just don't know if I have the strength to give them all they need from me. I don't know if I can be that version of Nancy anymore. Do you understand?"

Something in Janine's heart cracked. She reached across the table and gripped her mother's hand. They'd hardly touched since she had arrived on the island — only a few hugs here and there and almost no kind words. Surprise filled Nancy's face.

"Mom, I know it's been an awful year for you," Janine breathed. "But look at the life you built yourself. The woman I knew, all those years ago in New York City, is much different than the one I see before me."

Nancy dropped her eyes again as her cheeks flushed pink. Her shoulders fell forward as she whispered, "I am so ashamed. I never should have asked you to come here. I don't have anything to offer you. I can't help. Not at all." She then stood from her chair and turned toward the door, leaving Janine out on the porch alone.

Janine wasn't entirely sure what to do. Something about her mother, so broken at the table, told her to remain on the island to help her. Something told her that the Katama Lodge dream wasn't over, not yet.

They needed one another much more than either of them knew.

Janine walked over to the Katama Lodge and Wellness Spa after that. She found herself back in the foyer, watching as Carmella weaved in and out of the main room. Each time, she lifted a finger and said, "I should be able to find some time to talk in twenty minutes." But twenty minutes, then another twenty came and went, and Janine was becoming impatient.

Janine walked through the hallway, back toward where her mother and Neal's office had been. She wasn't sure what led her there. Maybe she just wanted to see more proof of her mother's "professional" life, as it still seemed so foreign.

Inside the office, there was a large photograph of Neal and Nancy on the wall. In it, Nancy wore a cream-colored dress, maybe even her wedding dress, while Neal wore a suit. They stood on a sailboat smiling, the very one Nancy had taken Janine out on. Nancy looked sinfully beautiful, as though all those years of drinking and sorrows had been washed away due to all the love she'd experienced there on the island.

"Did you remember me here?" Janine whispered to the photograph. "Did you want your only daughter to attend your wedding?"

Of course, Janine had been pretty clear in her opinion of her mother that last time she'd come to Manhattan. "Don't come back. I never want to see you again."

Yet here she was.

Janine stepped behind the desk and sat in the cushy chair. The desk had been organized and wiped clean.

There was a collection of folders off to the right, which seemed to contain information about the spa's various packages. Janine had already dreamed up her ideal schedule there at the lodge: what she would specialize in and how she would help these women get back on their feet.

With every step forward they took, she knew she, too, would heal.

Something caught the corner of Janine's eye after that. It was a dark cardboard box, clearly worn-down from age, and on the side, someone had written "NYC" in marker. She bent down to pull it out from under the desk as her heart pounded. As she lifted it into the air, she could almost see this very box, beneath another desk, far away in one of their Brooklyn apartments.

Was this possibly the same box? Had Nancy dragged it around the world with her, while she'd gallivanted, before winding up here?

At the very top of the box, Janine found a number of letters. She unfolded the first to find her own handwriting. The letter was dated 1997 — twenty-four years before.

Mom,

I don't think you'll even get this letter. Last I heard, Marvin told me you were in North Carolina, but I know you've been moving around a lot.

I don't know why you left the way you did. Yes, I know you couldn't pay our rent anymore, but Mom, I was only eighteen — hadn't even graduated from high school yet. And I still needed you so much.

The letter you left me, saying that you just needed to get well, totally destroyed me, Mom. I mean, there are options for you to get well here, with me.

*But actually, I'm writing this to tell you I'm not bitter
anymore. In fact, I've met someone — someone who will
protect me in ways you never could.*

Probably, you'll hear about me. He's famous.

*Anyway, I don't know why I'm writing any of this to
you because I'm nineteen now, and you've been gone an
entire year, and I don't even know where you are. Maybe
you're here. Maybe you're in Oregon or Illinois or Arizona
or any of the other fifty states. Maybe you ran off to Europe,
the way you always said you would if you had money.*

*Don't come find me. Although I've forgiven you, I will
never forget all you did.*

Janine

Janine's hands quivered as she read the letter. Tears
dripped down her cheeks, and she felt the lump lodged in
her throat. She didn't remember writing this letter,
although she could still feel the person she'd been back
then. So wounded but so sure of herself! So positive that
everything would work out!

Gosh, it hurt to read it.

Janine continued to dig through the various letters
and then found probably fifty photographs toward the
bottom. Most of them were of her, of Janine, at various
ages. She was seated in front of a large chocolate birthday
cake in only a diaper. Chocolate frosting was all around
her mouth, and she grinned madly at the camera — with
that knowledge only a toddler has, that they can get away
with murder. Then there was a photo of a much younger
Nancy, with Janine in her arms. They stood outside the
Brooklyn YMCA, where they sometimes had slept, and
the sun beat down upon them. Janine frowned in the
photo, but Nancy's smile was as big as her glasses at the
time. It was such a classic, early eighties photo.

There were others. Janine on a bicycle. Janine with her mother's lipstick on. Janine with her arms wrapped tightly around Maxine, her hair in pigtails. Janine was the central focus of the photos, but they all told a singular story — one of a young girl, who absolutely adored her mother, and a mother, who loved her girl so, so much but just couldn't keep herself together.

She just couldn't keep it together.

Suddenly, there was a knock on the door. Carmella appeared, then stopped short at the sight of Janine, whose face was probably so blotchy, so red, and heavy with tears.

"What's wrong? What happened to you?" Carmella breathed.

Janine dropped her face forward and let out a big sob. Carmella rushed around and wrapped her arms around her, then blinked down at the photos and whispered, "Oh my God. Look at these."

"I can't believe she kept them after all this time. After all the times I told her that I never wanted to see her again," Janine whispered.

After a long pause and several more sobs, Janine exhaled. "We can't give up on her, Carmella. No matter how complicated your feelings are with your father and sister. We have to keep going. She called me back to her. And I have to make things right."

Chapter Eighteen

Since Janine and Henry's little trek through Edgartown, Henry had texted Janine intermittently with updates about his documentary and its progression. He seemed busy, as his mother had only passed away in April, and he had a number of family responsibilities to tend to. Janine didn't mind, though. Time slipped through her fingers, and her heart still ached with sadness at what she'd lost. She wasn't exactly in the "mood" to flirt, not even with attractive, talented men like Henry. Friendship was all she needed.

At least, this is what she told herself. When she did hear from him again, the evening after she discovered the photographs and old letters in her mother's old office, her heart jumped into her throat and performed a little dance.

> HENRY: Hey! How are you? You haven't escaped the island for the city again, have you?

> JANINE: Nope. Still here.

She pressed send and then stared at their text conversations for a number of minutes. Panic set in. Had she not said enough? What were the rules of texting? It was way too soon to ask her daughters about such topics.

> JANINE: And how is the documentary coming?

Henry wrote back almost instantly. While the app showed him typing away, Janine didn't dare breathe. She felt like a teenager.

> HENRY: It's good. Better than before. The interviews gave me a better direction.

> HENRY: I just need to put more of my mom into it somehow. She was such a pillar in the Vineyard community.

Janine pressed her phone against her chest and again thought of the tremendous amount of loss they'd all experienced.

> JANINE: Can I ask you a question? In person.

> HENRY: I'm intrigued.

> JANINE: Don't worry. It's not an aggressive question or anything. I just might need your help.

> HENRY: No problem. This is the least busy summer of my life. I think I can find the time.

Henry and Janine agreed to meet the following afternoon. Henry suggested a little wine bar located near the Joseph Sylvia State Beach. As Janine approached, her skirt fluttered beautifully over her thighs and upper calves, and she tried and failed to tame her long locks, which flew wherever the wind took them.

Henry stood from one of the front tables, closer to the boardwalk. Janine's heart pounded at the sight of him. He looked cool, like the "artist from New York," with his dark jeans, black T-shirt, and untamed hair. His eyes met hers, and he looked genuinely happy to see her — her alone and no one else. Janine tried to remember what she'd first thought of Henry all those years ago when she'd first met him. Had she taken any interest in him?

No. She hadn't been that kind of woman. It had been Jack, and Jack only, for so long.

They ordered a bottle of wine. Janine was surprised at how frightened she was to make good conversation. She asked Henry what he'd been up to, and he spoke a bit more about his interviews, about his father's sadness, about his sisters, who both had remained on the island while he'd "run around the world."

"They must be impressed with everything you've done," Janine tried.

Henry laughed good-naturedly. "They just don't understand it. They know my films haven't been seen by so many people."

"That's the nature of art these days, I guess."

"You'd have to be sort of an idiot to get into the field," he said.

"No way. Just idealistic, I guess. Which is something we all need a little bit more of," Janine returned. She then sipped her wine and gazed out across the water. "Although, I'm really one to talk. I have to scrape my idealism from the bottom of the barrel."

"You seem to be doing remarkably," Henry said softly.

Janine shrugged. "I don't know. My main goal right now is to help my mother. She brought me here under the guise of helping me, but I think she needs my help more than ever. I want to help her reopen the Katama Lodge and Wellness Spa. I want to run it with her and her step-daughters. But she doesn't want to reopen. I need to figure out a way to make her see how important that place was for so many."

"I see." Henry's eyes widened. "And you thought about the interviews."

"Exactly." Janine was amazed that he read her mind so easily. "Maybe with some of the islanders who loved the Lodge the most. I've already spoken to several of these women. Their husbands died, or they got divorced, or they've had mild illness — and they found ways to rebuild at the lodge."

"I think that's fantastic," Henry said. "I'll help you, for sure."

"Really?" Janine's voice brightened a bit too much; she was reminded of a cheerleader. She cleared her throat and then added, "That would be so amazing."

"Don't mention it. Like I said, I have loads of time this summer. Time and a camera."

"Those just happen to be the two things I need the most."

* * *

Over the next few days, Janine and Henry spent nearly every waking moment together, conducting interviews with those who agreed to share their stories. First, they met with Mila, who Janine had met at the lodge itself. She explained her story again — how her husband, Peter, had died and how she'd taken refuge at the lodge to heal. She then passed along her best friends' names, including Jennifer Conrad of the Frosted Delights. When Janine entered the bakery, Jennifer beamed and said, "Mila already told me about your project. I would just love to help. You know how I feel about your mother. If you think she needs a push in the right direction, I'm here for you."

Jennifer's story weaved around her sister's death, again, along with the divorce from her high school sweetheart, Joel, whom she still loved dearly. "We've both moved on, and it's for the best, but I needed my time at the lodge after he moved out. I sat with these other, broken women, and we talked and talked for ages about everything. Of course, Nancy and Carmella's treatments were instrumental, as well."

Janine and Henry continued on across the island. They spoke briefly with a nurse named Carmella, who informed them that her husband had left her around the time of Neal's death, which meant she hadn't been able to go to the lodge during her time of need. "I would be there in a heartbeat if it was open," she told the camera. "Nancy, what you have in the lodge is truly remarkable. Don't forget that the women of Martha's Vineyard and beyond need you so much."

Their last stop of the day was at the Sunrise Cove Inn, where they spoke with a woman named Susan Sheridan. She reported that the previous year had been the turning point in her life. "I moved back to the Vineyard after twenty-five years away. I rekindled my relationships with my sisters and with my father. Then I found out I needed chemotherapy for breast cancer," she said into the camera. "After I found out that I'd been cured of cancer, I checked myself immediately into the lodge. I believe I was one of their last guests, and for that, I feel terribly lucky. Nancy, you do God's work there. I hope you know that."

They compiled twelve interviews with women from all walks of life. Excited, bubbling, Janine jumped into Henry's car and spoke endlessly about the various things people had said over the previous days while Henry drove them back to his quaint cabin, which he'd rented for his stay on the island. She was totally immersed in their project, as was he, so much so that she hardly questioned it. They both stood over his computer only an hour later and discussed how to edit the clips together, which parts could be deleted, and whether or not they should order pizza or Chinese food.

"Well, you know the Chinese here is nothing like the Chinese back home," Henry pointed out with a crooked grin.

"I'm sure you're right," Janine said, remembering her savory favorites from Chinatown restaurants. "I'm still craving it, though."

"Then I guess we'll make do," Henry said as he called the Edgartown Chinese restaurant, one that offered delivery.

An hour and a half later, they lay back, both of them with their hands over their overly-extended bellies. Throughout the night, they'd swapped stories about their time in Manhattan, about the various parties they had attended, and about which people they secretly detested in that "Manhattan socialite" circle.

"You have to understand, I was never really a part of it, like you," Henry said. "I was just there because Jack was sponsoring my film, and I hoped to meet other people who might throw me a bone later on down the line."

"I know that," Janine returned. "But you have to understand that I never really felt like I fit into that world either. I was just a poor girl from Brooklyn who struggled like so many others. And believe me; even after I met Jack, people went out of their way to let me know that's how they still saw me."

"That must have been awful." Henry tapped his chopsticks against the side of a paper box, which had held a savory, noodle-y concoction, nothing that even resembled anything from Chinatown.

"I sometimes think that previous version of myself might have paid anything to be here right now," Janine confessed then, surprising herself. "I haven't worn a designer dress in over a month. I haven't had my hair blown out or worried about what anyone thought of me. When I go out in public, I sometimes wear jeans. I never imagined how freeing it would be not to be Jack Potter's wife because I almost always had been. Now—"

She arched an eyebrow as the truth rolled off her tongue. *Was this really what she believed?*

It was.

Silence fell between them. Janine wondered if she'd pointed too firmly at some kind of truth and "freaked him out."

Finally, Henry answered.

"I think you're better off without him. I mean,

everyone always knew he wasn't the most loyal of husbands."

Janine dropped her chopsticks. She pressed herself back in her chair and gaped at Henry, who suddenly seemed like a stranger.

This was her life he spoke about.

This wasn't something to joke about.

Her heart darkened. As time passed, Henry tilted in his chair, seemingly confused.

"I'm sorry. Did I say something wrong?"

Janine swallowed the lump in her throat.

"I'm sorry. I just assumed, what with everything that happened, that you knew—"

"Knew it wasn't the first time?" Janine breathed.

Henry seemed unwilling to say yes or no to that. He just blinked at her.

"I guess I would be an idiot to think Maxine was the first time," she said then. "Maybe I am the idiot. It's the only thought that's run through my mind, nonstop, since I got here. Maybe I just ignored all the signs. My God, how stupid of me."

"Janine, don't."

But she'd already begun to get up, to grab her cardigan and her purse, to head for the door. Her shoulders shook as she rushed, and she found her way to Elsa's car swiftly, grateful that she'd allowed her to borrow it yet again. She turned on the engine as Henry stalled on the walkway that led from the driveway to the front door.

"Janine, please. Let me explain," he called, loud enough for her to hear through the window.

But Janine didn't want to talk about the past any longer. She drove as fast as she could down the road, all the way back to her mother's house. Once there, she stared long and hard at her mother's closed door. For the first time in thirty years, maybe, she considered crawling into her mother's bed, searching for comfort.

It was impossible, now.

Once in her bedroom, she checked her phone. Henry had sent her a number of messages.

> HENRY: I am so sorry, Janine.

> HENRY: I was completely out of line.

> HENRY: I should know when to put my foot in my mouth.

Janine exhaled slowly. She tried to fall into a meditative zone, unthinking, unfeeling, but soon jumped out of it into a state of panic.

Finally, she wrote him back.

> JANINE: It's my fault for being sensitive.

> JANINE: Thank you for your help the past few days. I love what we did with the videos, and I can't wait to show Nancy.

> JANINE: Really. I am sorry for freaking out. Jack is just a ghost, now. I hate that I still allow him to haunt me.

> HENRY: We all have our ghosts. It's a part of life.

> JANINE: Right now, I think my mother and I are haunting each other.

> HENRY: I think it's because you have unfinished business. It isn't over between you two. Not even close.

JANINE: You should write horror screenplays.

HENRY: I don't know about that. Real life is about as scary as it gets. It's why I'm a documentarian.

Chapter Nineteen

In the wake of Janine and Carmella's failed dinner with Nancy, Nancy spent as little time downstairs as she could. Janine hardly caught sight of Elsa, either — and when she did, Elsa seemed to try to scamper out of sight, as though she worried she, too, would be cornered about the future of the lodge. One morning, as Janine poured herself a cup of coffee quietly in the kitchen, Elsa entered and then looked on the verge of leaping right back out again.

"Good morning!" Janine said brightly. "I haven't seen you in a while. What have you been up to?"

Elsa grimaced slightly. Probably, she didn't trust Janine any longer, as she was clearly "in cahoots" with the sister she didn't get along with.

"Here and there, busy with the kids," Elsa said.

"Thanks again for letting me borrow the car the other day." Janine made heavy eye contact. She wanted to keep Elsa close. There was still so much she didn't know about the woman. She worried Elsa would never let her in.

"Not a problem." Elsa's tone made Janine feel like a stranger. She stepped toward the coffee pot and poured herself a mug, then turned her eyes toward the window.

"I'm worried about my mom." Janine's words were somber. "She spends all her days in that room."

"I see her," Elsa insisted. "I'm making sure she's okay."

Janine's heart dropped the slightest bit. "That's good to hear. Thank you."

They held the silence for a moment. Janine hesitated. She so wanted to apologize, but she wasn't entirely sure for what.

"I read about this Solstice Festival in Oak Bluffs," she said then.

Elsa nodded. "We have it every year."

"My daughters mentioned maybe coming to the island for it," Janine continued. "I want to tell Nancy that. That maybe she'll have a chance to meet her granddaughters properly. Do you think she'd be up for something like that?"

Elsa's eyes flashed with uncertainty. Again, she turned her eyes toward Janine's. "I'll talk to her."

Janine nodded. "Elsa, I know she mentioned maybe leaving the island, maybe leaving the lodge. But I don't think that's really the best thing for her. Do you?"

"I don't know. Nancy has to do what's right for her." Elsa's voice wavered, proof that she knew this line of thought, and it pained her. "I just want to offer her as much love and support as I can. I know what it's like to lose a husband. Some days, crawling out of bed is like climbing a mountain."

* * *

Janine was genuinely surprised that Maggie and Alyssa had agreed to meet her on Martha's Vineyard. On the morning of their arrival, she borrowed Elsa's car again and snaked over to Oak Bluffs to pick them up from the ferry. She stood out in the splendor of the summertime sun and watched as first, the long-legged Maggie, dressed in a perfect white dress, and then, Alyssa, dressed in a light pink frock, swept off the ferry and waved their slender arms. They were picture-perfect.

"Mom!" Maggie cried as she threw her arms around her, in the style of a much younger Maggie — a girl who didn't care about paparazzi or what people thought. "Look at you. You're so tan and fit."

Janine blushed as she turned to hug Alyssa next. "I'm just keeping myself busy. Not much else to do."

"Look at this place," Alyssa breathed as they collected the suitcases and headed toward where Janine had parked the car. "It's so quaint. Like a painting."

"It's kind of like living in a fictional universe," Janine admitted as she helped the girls assemble the suitcases in the back.

"Whose car is this, Mom?" Maggie asked.

"This is your step-aunt Elsa's car."

"Huh. Elsa. And you said there's another step-aunt, right?" Alyssa asked.

"Carmella. Although she keeps her distance."

"Why's that?" Alyssa asked.

"I'm not entirely sure yet. It seems like there were some problems in the past. A lot of bad blood," Janine offered.

They drove out toward Nancy's home, which Janine saw with fresh eyes, now that she had her daughters with her. She was conscious that her heart had ballooned four times its size, maybe, and that it took only a little comment like, *"Wow, look at that water!"* or, *"Looks like good hiking trails back there,"* for her to grin widely. She found herself really wanting her girls to like the Vineyard, despite this being one of the strangest eras of her life.

"Grandma lives here?" Maggie asked, surprised as Janine drew the car to a halt at the top of the driveway.

Janine reasoned that this mansion along the waterfront was a far cry from her descriptions of her and Nancy's life in Brooklyn. Probably it was all nonsensical to her daughters. It was for her, too.

"Neal was very prosperous with his lodge," Janine explained.

"Grandma married good!" Alyssa hopped out of the car as her hair flew with the wind.

As the girls assembled their suitcases outside the car, Nancy appeared on the porch. She wore a hat to shield her eyes, which were assuredly not so used to the sun after a week or so indoors, and she'd donned a white cardigan and a pair of slacks. She looked smaller and more skeletal than she had the week before. But when she lifted her hand in greeting and said, "Are those my beautiful granddaughters?" Janine's heart leaped into her throat with excitement.

This was a moment she would remember forever.

Alyssa and Maggie hustled up the steps and shrieked with joy. Nancy wrapped her arms around both of them and closed her eyes. "My girls! Look at you. Your both the spitting image of your mother when she was your age. All of you, such beauties!"

"I wonder where we get those genes, Grandma," Alyssa said brightly.

Nancy's eyes found Janine's, all the way down in the driveway. There was gratefulness behind her smile, along with surprise. Probably, she hadn't expected the girls to call her "grandma" so readily since Janine normally went with "Nancy."

But the joy that beamed out from Nancy's face told Janine to wean herself off that. This was her mother. It was time to give power to the word "mom."

Janine, Alyssa, Maggie, and Nancy gathered together on the back porch. Nancy poured them freshly-squeezed lemonade and spoke excitedly, asking her granddaughters what they'd been up to over the previous few weeks of early summer.

"Maggie, your mom, showed me photos of you and your fiancé," Nancy said conspiratorially. "I have to say; he's one of the most handsome men I've seen in my life!"

Maggie giggled. "He's not only handsome. He's actually genuinely kind."

"A rare breed, then," Nancy offered knowingly.

Maggie tilted her head and grinned wider. "You have to come to the wedding, Grandma. Really."

Nancy's lips formed a round O, as though she'd never imagined such an invitation. Her eyes found Janine's as Janine nodded firmly.

"It would be a complete honor to be there," Nancy whispered as her eyes glowed.

"It will be the most exciting celebration," Alyssa interjected playfully. "Princess Maggie wants everything perfect."

Maggie laughed. "I'm not a bridezilla, Alyssa."

"You already changed your mind about the invitations four times, and you refuse to buy a wedding dress, even though we've looked at so many," Alyssa pointed out.

Maggie arched an eyebrow toward Janine. "I told you. I want to wait till Mom gets back to the city."

Suddenly, Nancy clapped her hands together and said, "One of my dear friends on the Vineyard is a wedding dress designer! Perhaps we can meet her while you girls are here."

Maggie looked doubtful, even as her voice rang out to say, "Oh, maybe..."

But before the doubt could ring too true, Nancy grabbed her phone and began to show Maggie the gowns her friend, Greta, had created for a number of celebrities, daughters of diplomats and politicians, and other rich folk from both on and off the Vineyard.

Maggie was captivated. She gripped Nancy's phone as her eyes widened. "That detail! It's insane that she makes this with her own two hands."

"She's a magician," Nancy affirmed.

Maggie flipped through to more designs and then gasped. "I didn't know she was the designer for Thelma Tipperton! I went to that wedding, and I almost went crazy for her dress."

"She really did," Alyssa said. "She wouldn't shut up about it."

Nancy's eyes found Janine's, as she gave a little, playful shrug and said, "I guess I'd better give Greta a call?"

"Please do, Grandma!" Maggie cried, with her hands steepled beneath her chin, like she was praying.

Within the next ten minutes, Nancy had arranged a brief stop-over with her longtime friend, Greta, who'd apparently said, "If your granddaughter wants a dress, I will go out of my way to make her one, Nancy."

At this news, Maggie clasped her hands over her

mouth and gasped. "I can't believe it. Grandma, this is crazy. Mom, you didn't tell me Grandma was so connected."

Janine eyed her mother knowingly as Nancy blushed. "You're a woman of infinite secrets, Mom," Janine commented. "Who knows what you'll reveal to us next?"

Nancy beamed.

It was decided that they would meet with Greta, the wedding dress designer, the following afternoon. In the meantime, they prepared for the Solstice Festival in Oak Bluffs. Maggie and Alyssa decided to change into alternate dresses for the night, leaving Janine and Nancy downstairs alone. Silence filled the space between them, but it was a comfortable silence, a time that didn't make Janine twitch with fear.

"Your girls are something special," Nancy said softly as they continued to hear Alyssa and Maggie's voices ring out from the guest room.

"They really are. They're the best of me," Janine breathed.

"You kept them grounded, despite the world they grew up in," Nancy said knowingly. "You can feel it in everything they say. They're grateful and kind and intelligent."

Janine's voice broke. "It means so much to hear you say that. Really. I—"

But before she could answer, Alyssa and Maggie appeared at the base of the stairs, ready to hit the road. Nancy just nodded. There was more light and color to her cheeks than there'd been in the previous week.

Maybe there really was something to this "family needs to stick together" stuff.

The Solstice Festival was located along the waterline,

in full view of numerous, ever-tilting sailboats, the ferry dock, and the old-world carousel, which was a historic landmark that had been moved from New York City to Martha's Vineyard back in the 1880s.

"That carousel is similar to both of you, Mom and Grandma," Alyssa said brightly. "It moved here from the city to get away from it all."

Janine and Nancy held one another's gaze for a moment and then laughed. Maybe this was the right way.

Nancy flourished in this environment, just as she had a few weeks before. Janine watched, captivated, as Nancy introduced her Vineyard friends to her beautiful grand-daughters. She bragged endlessly about Maggie's engagement and Alyssa's recent graduation from Yale.

"They look just like you and Janine," several people said as they donned large smiles. "You girls have strong genes."

Alyssa, Maggie, Janine, and Nancy walked through the festival, then ended up near the water, seated beneath a tent where they served wine and light snacks. From where they were, they could feast on the light pinks and oranges of the sunset as it glossed across the waters. They were also close enough to the live music to enjoy it while still hearing one another. Janine shivered, not because she was chilly, but because she felt totally safe and happy. When silence fell, Maggie reached across the table, gripped Janine's hand, and said, "I just can't get over how great this place is. It's got this whole community feel that I've never experienced in the city."

"Stay as long as you like!" Nancy cried.

The Grimson-Remington-Potter women sipped their glasses of wine and fell into gossip. Janine's heart surged with love for them. Alyssa told a story of a recent date she'd gone on with a Wall Street executive. "He was the most boring man I've ever met, maybe," she said, as Nancy burst into laughter. Maggie then spoke about her fiancé, about his insistence that they always buy cheap burritos from the burrito truck down the road. "We used to go to five-star restaurants all the time, and now, all he wants is a cheesy burrito from the corner to be eaten on the couch while we watch TV," Maggie said as she rolled her eyes.

"Men are the same everywhere," Nancy said with a laugh. "They just want to eat and laze around."

"I can't fault them for that. I feel exactly the same," Alyssa added as she lifted her glass of wine. "Hope I find my eating soul mate soon!"

Nancy giggled. "Neal knew how to snack with the best of them. A few months before he died, he came to bed with all these crackers and fancy cheeses, and we had a little feast while we watched reruns. I sometimes felt like we were much younger when we were together."

"It should be like that," Maggie said as her eyes widened. "It should always feel like you're discovering new things together. Right? Even new ways of snacking."

"I always thought so," Nancy said. Her eyes glistened with tears, but she seemed to manage to hold them back. "I wish you girls could have met him. He was a remarkable human. Really. He changed my life. Before that — I don't know. Maybe your mother told you. Probably she has. I wasn't such a good person."

Silence fell over the four of them for a moment — three generations of women, all living out a very different storyline. Suddenly, Janine reached across the table and gripped her mother's hand. How could she possibly translate how much she wanted to move forward? How much she needed happiness in her life? How much she needed her mother for the first time in decades?

Chapter Twenty

That night, Janine slipped beneath the sheets of her bed and fell back against the pillows. Her head spun with a kaleidoscope of stories, all from the remarkable lips of her daughters and her mother, and her heart swelled with love for all of them. Even toward the end of the night, when they'd again sat around the porch table at the house, Elsa had arrived home and joined them, grateful for a glass of wine and a bit of laughter. Alyssa and Maggie had brought light and joy to the house, a house that had been shrouded in so much darkness, and for the first time since Janine had met her, Elsa had cracked several jokes. She found ways to bring out her personality, maybe even the personality she'd lost in the wake of her husband and father's deaths.

That moment, there was a slight rap on the door. Janine furrowed her brow, dropped her foot to the side of the bed, and then walked through the darkness. When she opened the door, she discovered her mother there with two mugs of steaming hot chocolate and a soft smile on her lips.

"Mom," Janine breathed.

Nancy lifted the mugs and said, "Do you mind if I come in for a second? I want to talk about something."

Janine turned on the lamp and led her mother back toward the bed. They sat together and turned their eyes toward the blanket between them. Without Alyssa and Maggie, their buffers, it seemed they were doomed for awkwardness.

"I remember when you used to make hot cocoa for me when I was little," Janine said suddenly. "When I couldn't sleep."

"When we lived next to those noisy neighbors," Nancy whispered. "I remember that. They fought all through the night."

Janine's heart dropped at the memory. There, so close to the waves, surrounded by these thick walls, in the softness of her mother's love, such darkness and pain seemed so far away.

"I can't tell you how much it meant to me today, spending time with those girls," Nancy whispered. "I know I don't deserve to have a relationship with them. Or you."

Janine swallowed a lump in her throat.

"I put you through more pain and torment than any child should have ever gone through," Nancy continued. "And then, when I thought maybe you could handle yourself, I left without even a thought about how you might manage on your own. I figured you could take care of yourself much better than I could at that point. I think I was even right about that, since I was such a mess. Always with the wrong man. Always drinking a little too much. Never having enough money. I was a walking hurricane."

Janine was on the verge of tears. This was the first her

mother had said of any of this since her arrival. It felt strangely good to hear it all; finally, it was an acknowledgment that they'd spent all that time together at all, that they'd gone through so much pain.

"I thought you were okay for so long, you know?" Nancy breathed. "I would check up on you over the years. See you in various tabloids or fashion magazines. Always hear how you were this humble girl with this princess life. I was so proud of you."

"And now? Now that he's left me?" Janine exhaled as her voice cracked.

Nancy shook her head somberly. "I don't think about him at all. I see only a beautiful, profound human being before me. Someone who carries herself well, despite everything she's endured. Someone who raised remarkable daughters and someone who left when it was time to leave. Here you are. And maybe, just maybe, you'll find it in your heart to forgive me."

Janine's heart broke in two. She could feel the tears run down her cheeks when she finally looked up at her mother and murmured, "I already have, Mom."

"Oh, honey." Nancy closed her eyes tightly and heaved a sigh as she pulled her daughter in for a hug. They both relished the warmth of being in each other's arms for a moment before finally letting go.

Nancy looked at Janine. "I need to ask you if you would still be willing to help me reopen the lodge. I know I wasn't so keen on it the other day. But you're right. The act of helping all these women heal has always helped to heal me, too. I think it's the only thing we can do. We have to keep going. We have to guide each other back to the light."

Janine shivered. "Do you think Elsa will be okay with it?"

"I'll talk to her tomorrow," Nancy returned. "Ultimately, Neal left the lodge to me. And God knows Elsa needs something to live for right now. When I look her in the eye, I see so much sadness. You should have known her before her husband died. Goodness, we were thick as thieves, the two of us. She always knew that I missed you — that I wanted my daughter back. And she was always sensitive to that. But she helped me through. I owe her so much."

"I want to know her. I hope she'll let me," Janine said softly.

That afternoon, Nancy, Janine, Alyssa, and Maggie gathered at the wedding dress designer's mansion just outside of Oak Bluffs and discussed wedding dress logistics with Greta. Greta doted on Maggie in every way, and Maggie beamed excitedly, discussed the various styles she liked, and turned her eye toward Janine frequently as she asked her opinion. "What do you think of this, Mom?" and "Mom, do you think this would work?"

When the girls left the designer's house, they gathered outside a little restaurant along the waterline and ordered some merlot. There, Janine and Nancy made eye contact and said, almost in unison, "We have something to tell you."

"What is it?" Alyssa asked brightly.

"Okay, should we be worried?" Maggie demanded, arching a brow.

Nancy exhaled slowly and then lifted her glass of

wine. "We've decided to reopen the Katama Lodge and Wellness Spa. Me, your mom, along with your aunt Elsa and aunt Carmella."

"Seriously?!" Maggie cried.

"That's fantastic! Mom, you're going to work again! Grandma, Mom was absolutely crazy for her naturopathic practice," Alyssa continued. "We couldn't believe it when you closed the place down."

Janine, who'd long since given up on fully comprehending why she'd closed her practice, lifted her glass and beamed. "I can't wait to get back to it."

"When do you think you'll reopen?" Alyssa asked.

"I spoke with Elsa this morning, and she thinks we could even be booked up for the Fourth of July," Nancy said.

"That's just around the corner!" Maggie cried.

"Do you need any help reopening the place?" Alyssa arched an eyebrow.

"Oh, you girls probably have so much going on," Nancy said. "You don't need to reserve any mental space for the Katama Lodge."

"Come on. We'd love to help," Maggie affirmed. "Put us to work. You don't have long before the Fourth."

Janine and Nancy made eye contact and then burst into laughter. They'd already marveled that the Fourth of July was much, much too soon — but that crazier things had happened.

"Maybe, if you'd be willing to come back next weekend, maybe we can put you to work," Nancy said with a wide grin. "But we'll pay you back with buckets of wine and delicious seafood."

"That sounds like a good deal to me," Alyssa said.

* * *

The next few weeks were a blur. Janine found herself in the midst of the chaos, constantly writing to-do lists, making runs to the hardware store, and getting down on her hands and knees to scrub and dust and investigate different areas of the Lodge to make sure everything was prepared for the upcoming guests.

Elsa, who'd always been in charge of branding, social media, and general reservations for the lodge and spa, announced around June 25th that they were already booked up for all of July. Janine and Nancy, who were both bleary-eyed and exhausted from their nonstop cleaning and organizing, suddenly found the energy to jump up and down in celebration. Elsa popped open a bottle of champagne, and the three of them enjoyed a glass as the sun set in a gooey haze of pink.

"We're really back," Elsa whispered. "And I think Dad would be so proud of us. I really do."

"Your dad wouldn't have wanted us to mope around for the rest of our lives," Nancy affirmed. "He believed in the lodge. And the best thing we can do to sustain his memory is to keep it going."

The following weekend, just as they'd promised, Alyssa and Maggie arrived at the Vineyard to help out with the Lodge. Janine had never seen her daughters work so hard. They helped prepare the bedrooms of the lodge, made lists for various food items the kitchen would need for their grand reopening on the Fourth, and even started to organize the elaborate party, which they'd decided to have on the Fourth of July itself, in order to kick-start excitement for the lodge. Much of the island was invited, including all of the women Janine and Henry interviewed for their project.

Janine frequently thought of Henry. As she fell deeper in with the Lodge and its preparations, she felt further and further away from him and sensed that he, too, had found new ways to fill his time. She hoped that his documentary had continued to morph and change. She hoped that he'd begun to make peace with his mother's death.

It wasn't as though they could fall in love or anything like that. Her separation from Jack was too recent, and her pain was still too great. Maybe, in a month or two or six, she and Henry could continue the path of friendship. Or maybe, he'd go back to the city, where he wanted to belong, and she would continue there with her mother.

Despite everything, Janine did think of Henry almost every time she passed by the Edgartown Lighthouse. Her heart ached with longing as she remembered those people, over one hundred years ago, who'd gathered on that long-lost Bridge of Sighs and watched their loved ones being taken away on whaling expeditions. How tremendously horrible to say goodbye to those you loved — yet wasn't it somehow a part of life? Those who truly mattered had always found a way back to you. And maybe, in that way, it was proof that their love was the strongest of all.

Chapter Twenty One

Janine arrived at the Katama Lodge and Wellness Spa on the morning of the Fourth of July. She wore a white dress, which scooped toward her breasts beautifully, and her hair was full and curly and shining beneath the glowing light of an ever-present sun. When she stepped into the foyer, she discovered Carmella at the front desk, positively beaming at her.

"There she is," Carmella greeted. "The woman who made this all happen."

Janine laughed. "I don't know about that. I couldn't have done any of this without you. And Mom. And Elsa."

Carmella stepped around the front desk and leaned heavily against it. She crossed her arms over her chest and said, "You know, it's difficult for people to realize just how much impact they have on others. I think we feel that way sometimes in these naturopathic fields, as well. Acupuncture, spa treatments, all of it — it really does create lasting effects in these women. And in the same way, I don't want you to discredit what you've done here. You gave your mother a reason to keep going."

Janine blushed and brought a strand of hair behind her ear. There was still so much she didn't understand about this world. So much she didn't know about Carmella and Elsa and the entire Remington family. Even through the reopening and party-planning process, Elsa and Carmella had hardly spoken to one another. Maggie had commented on it the previous weekend, stating, "You have to get to the bottom of what's up between Carmella and Elsa. I can't imagine if Alyssa and I got into some kind of fight like that. They won't even look at each other."

Janine and Carmella stepped out onto the back porch, which overlooked the water. There, they watched as several workers, all of whom they'd recently hired for various everyday operations at the Lodge, lifted a large white tent toward the sky. Tables would be set up beneath this, and a dance floor would stretch from beneath the tent toward the water. A local band had been hired, along with a famous caterer, Zach Walters, who generally worked for the Sunrise Cove Bistro over in Oak Bluffs.

"I can't wait to get my hands on that food," Carmella said now with a laugh. "The food at the bistro is to die for, and Zach is a difficult guy to book. I can't believe you managed it."

Janine blushed. "Back in Manhattan, I was pretty good at planning parties. It turned into my whole life, especially after I quit my practice."

"You're good at it," Carmella pointed out. "But I have to imagine you're pretty damn good at everything."

Janine blushed. "Since everything happened, I haven't felt particularly good at anything."

"The Lodge will help," Carmella said softly as her eyes caught the light off the water. "I have a feeling that all good things are about to begin—for all of us in the Remington-Grimson-Potter household."

Janine grimaced. "I think it's about time I drop the Potter name." She swallowed then and wrapped her hands around the back porch railing. "I don't feel him here, you know. Jack. He was so much a part of Manhattan. Everyone knew his name, and everyone knew me by extension. But here, I'm just Janine. I'm Nancy's daughter. I don't have any association with big cocktail parties, gossip circles, or stupid tabloid magazines. I even stopped checking the online gossip columnists because I realized I don't care at all what's said about me. I feel like I'm finally free."

The Fourth of July party at the Katama Lodge and Wellness Spa began just after six in the evening. Smells of barbecue, platters of seafood and glorious freshly baked bread and pies swirled out from the kitchen and through the tent, mixing with the smells of the salty ocean and the beautiful trees surrounding the property on all sides. Janine stood with her mother for the first hour or so, toward the front of the property, to greet Vineyard residents and locals, all of whom expressed their gratitude and excitement that the Katama Lodge was reopened.

Carmella stationed herself in the foyer downstairs throughout the early part of the party, as the women who'd set aside the holiday week to spend time and heal at the Katama Lodge itself had already begun to check in. They'd been told about the party, and they hurriedly dropped off their things in their suites, changed clothes, and then met with one another in the big tent for dinner and drinks.

Janine met several of these women, some of whom had traveled from as far away as Oregon and Arizona.

"I came to the Katama Lodge ten years ago," one woman said excitedly. "I worked directly with Carmella and another of the naturopathic residents here. I had just lost my sister to cancer, and I was struggling so much. After that, I found the strength to keep going. When I saw that the Lodge was reopening, I knew I had to come back for a kind of check-in with myself. And look at that view! I swear the Bay has never looked better. After all these years, it's like I can feel all the previous versions of myself right here."

Maggie and Alyssa arrived at the party around seven. Their excitement was overzealous, and they hugged Nancy and Janine and jumped up at down at the beautiful party, the boisterous band, the wonderful food, and the hanging lights, which made the yard simmer with magic and the large pool glisten with its glow.

Janine spotted Nancy on the back porch, overlooking the party, as the first of the evening light was cast over everyone else. Janine stepped up beside her mother and followed her gaze over the revelers. Laughter and conversation bubbled up throughout the crowd. It took a long time, but finally, Nancy exhaled softly and said, "I just can't believe this. Neal would be so pleased with how it turned out."

Janine's throat tightened. "I can't imagine what it must feel like to move forward without him."

Nancy shifted her gaze toward her daughter. "He would laugh so much, I think."

"About what?"

"All those years, I cried about you. I wanted to find a way back to you. A way to ask you to return to me. Maybe he would say — *look, Nancy. You needed me out of the way so you could get your first real love back."* Nancy's eyes sparkled. "That would be the kind of thing that would make him laugh a lot. He would say it was all meant to be."

Janine swallowed, unsure of what to say. After a long pause, she said, "Carmella says everyone checked in for the night. We're off to the races tomorrow. I have my first appointment at ten in the morning. And they continue throughout the day."

Nancy gripped Janine's hand hard over the railing. "These women don't know how much you're about to change their lives."

Janine's heart swelled. "I hope I'm up for it."

"You will be," Nancy said.

Suddenly, out of the corner of her eye, Janine caught sight of a familiar man. He waded through the crowd down below as the haze of orange evening light toyed with his dark, curly head of hair. It had been weeks since Janine had seen any sign of Henry, and she was surprised that a lump caught in her throat and her stomach fluttered with butterflies.

"I have to go speak with someone," Janine said suddenly. "But I'll be back."

"Take your time, Janine," Nancy said. "You created a beautiful party. You should be allowed to enjoy it."

"The hostess's job is never complete." Janine beamed as she stepped away. "But here, those mean Manhattan socialites don't have their eyes on me at all times. I can probably take a few minutes for myself."

"Absolutely," Nancy said brightly.

Janine was in such a rush that she took the steps two at a time and hustled through the crowd. When she reached Henry, he was faced away from her. She lifted a finger and tapped him on the shoulder, and he immediately stepped around so that his eyes grabbed hold of hers. They gazed at one another. Janine's tongue felt suddenly heavy. She had absolutely nothing to say. She just wanted to stand there beside him. It was the simplest feeling in the world.

"Hey there," she said.

"Hi."

Janine swallowed and then gestured out across the party. "I'm surprised you came by."

"Heard about it through the grapevine," Henry said. "Small island and all."

"That it is."

"But it's beautiful. The party, I mean," Henry offered.

"Thank you."

"Not that you weren't always brilliant at planning parties," Henry affirmed.

Janine's throat constricted again. She glanced up toward the back porch, where her mother remained.

"How did you convince her to go through with it?" Henry finally asked. "To reopen, I mean."

Janine shrugged. "Something changed. I think she realized that there was so much love between us. And that I wasn't willing to give up on it, just because there was so much darkness in our past."

"That's beautiful," Henry said.

"I know it's going to be a hard road, but we're both up for it. I guess, what else is there to do but work for it?"

"Well said." Henry leafed through his pocket and

then drew out a USB stick. "I wanted to bring you the video we made together. It's a great record of what your mother has done here over the years."

Janine's lips parted in shock. She hadn't expected Henry to go ahead and finish editing the video without her, especially after their little spat. It was the kindest of all gestures, without any kind of reward.

"Thank you. This is incredible," Janine said softly. She slipped the USB into her own pocket and continued to gaze into his eyes. "And how is your project going?"

Henry hesitated. "To be honest, it's taken a back seat to a few family issues. I've really gotten to know my sisters again in recent weeks. And my father and I even went fishing together the other day."

"Wow. The elusive Henry is reconnecting with his Vineyard roots," Janine teased tenderly.

"It seems like it," Henry said. "And I have to admit. I don't hate it as much as I always thought I would. I thought I might stick it out over the summer, maybe even into the autumn. Be the son my father always dreamed of. Be there for my sisters and my nieces and nephews. I don't know. Maybe this place has given me a new sense of myself and my creativity. Maybe I don't want to throw that away just yet."

Janine slipped a strand of hair behind her ear. She suddenly felt girlish and silly. "The island is better with you on it, I think."

"I think everyone here would agree with that senti-ment when it comes to you being here," Henry returned.

At that moment, there was the screech of a micro-phone. Janine glanced up to find Elsa, center-stage, near where the band stepped back to allow her to speak.

"Thank you, each and every one of you, for coming

out to welcome us back to the fold," Elsa announced. "I know that in the wake of the lodge's closing, my heart has been a little sadder, a little emptier. I was so resistant to reopen because I wasn't sure how we could manage it without my dear dad. But together, with the help of my beautiful stepmother, stepsister, and along with my sister, Carmella..."

She said this last part doubtfully.

"We've managed to do it," Elsa continued. "Thank you, to this wonderful and generous island, for welcoming us back in true Vineyard fashion. We love you. Thank you for your support. And happy Fourth of July! Let's keep this party going!"

Everyone in the crowd hollered and hooted and clapped their hands. Elsa introduced the band back to the stage, and they soon rollicked into a rousing version of "God Bless America" while they all watched fireworks go off over the water.

Henry's eyes flashed as he returned his gaze to Janine's.

"Do you know much about Elsa's and Carmella's past?" he asked suddenly.

Janine's heart dropped. "I know there's a lot of darkness."

Henry nodded. "Did you know they had a brother?"

News of this sliced Janine right through her belly. "Had? He died?"

"It was really tragic," Henry said. "The island mourned for a long, long time. But also, then their mother died — and then Neal remarried a few years later. She was a really evil woman."

Shock sizzled through Janine's stomach. She turned her eyes back toward Elsa, who stepped off the stage and walked directly past Carmella. Janine felt it again: the heaviness of their past, so much she couldn't understand or see. It went deep beyond words.

"Anyway. I just wanted to drop this off," Henry said. "I had better head out. I told my sister I'd be back."

"Thank you, Henry," Janine said. She felt the USB in her pocket. "I can't tell you what this means to me."

"Don't mention it," Henry returned. "I'll see you around now that you're an islander."

He winked and then disappeared through the crowd. Janine's heart pounded strangely as she watched him go. Something told her that her life wasn't over yet. It was only just beginning.

Chapter Twenty-Two

It was a strange thing, falling into the rhythm of the Katama Lodge and Wellness Spa. Even after only a few days, Janine was amazed at the clockwork-like ease with which she, Carmella, Nancy, Elsa, and the other workers at the lodge worked alongside one another. The space was comfortable and quiet, with soft, relaxing music easing through the halls. The food from the restaurant area was mostly vegan, all simmering with nutrients and all absolutely divine, created with the masterstroke recipe work of a nutritionist Nancy and Janine had hired from the West Coast.

As Janine walked the halls and through the tables in the dining area, she heard snippets of conversations from their guests.

"That acupuncture from Carmella yesterday? It totally relaxed me. Last night, I had the best night's sleep I've had in years. I feel like a little kid."

"I have Carmella later this afternoon. But earlier this morning, Janine prescribed me a very particular diet. She said my exhaustion is probably hormonal, and I'm not eating enough of these vitamins. She gave me this chart. Look."

"I did yoga by the pool with Nancy at sunrise. The woman is almost sixty years old, and she has some of the best flexibility I've seen in my life."

"She also looks so much younger than sixty."

"Did you know Nancy and Janine are mother and daughter?"

"What! I mean, they look similar..."

"Someone said that Nancy had Janine when she was like sixteen or something."

"That's crazy. Can you imagine growing up, having Nancy as your mother? It must have been incredible."

"An adventure, every single day."

"And so much meditation. I wonder if she taught Janine everything she knows?"

"I read the pamphlet, and it looks like Janine studied separately from Nancy."

"Huh. Well, they were certainly drawn to this same discipline for a reason."

* * *

Janine loved her one-on-one time with her clients. She often spoke with them for up to two hours, and they covered almost everything, from what they ate in a day to what they did for exercise, to what their relationship was like with their parents and children and siblings, to how they saw themselves as individuals.

It was this way that Janine came to understand that many, many of the women who stayed at the lodge were in the middle of seriously tumultuous times.

"We just can't get pregnant," one woman told her

somberly, her eyes toward her clasped hands. "We've been trying for five years. Jimmy said that maybe, we should adopt? I feel like such a failure. I keep thinking, if only I eat something different, or exercise more, or think differently, or even pray better, we'll be given the gift of a baby. But that baby isn't coming, and it's like, every day that passes, I feel Jimmy moving further and further away from me."

"My husband started having an affair when I was pregnant with our third child," another woman said. "I knew it was happening, and a part of me didn't even care since I had these two babies to take care of on top of my pregnant self. But when I looked into his eyes, I saw nothing there. None of the love I thought I'd married into."

"My father died last year. We were never close, but I found that the news hit me so hard, as though a bomb had gone off in my heart. I couldn't eat properly for a while. Then I couldn't sleep without dreaming of him and all the regrets I had around our time together, or lack of it."

Hour by hour, day after day, the women at the Katama Lodge began to reveal themselves to Janine, and Janine answered in turn — using diagnostic tests to understand their health conditions, prescribing them acupuncture and various holistic medicines, and asking that they treat themselves to a number of spa treatments and massages there at the lodge and spa.

Every woman revealed the density and beauty of their inner souls.

Every woman seemed to have so much they still wanted to give the world, yet struggled, as they still carried around so much pain.

On July 12th, Janine walked toward her mother's yoga

studio within the lodge itself. She stood at the doorway and peered inside as her mother finished up her class of only five women, all of whom had wrapped themselves into the child's pose. Nancy stood at the head of the room, close to the windows, and placed her palms together.

"Here, you feel calm. Reunite yourselves with your inner child. Remember where you felt safest, most at peace, and go there in your mind. Breathe. Breathe."

Nancy's eyes found Janine's. She bowed her head and smiled, just the slightest bit.

When Nancy dismissed the women for dinner, Janine and Nancy stood together near the far end of the room and gazed out toward the water. Both of them seemed speechless. Janine, who'd had back-to-back appointments with clients, was exhausted yet completely thrilled.

"This has really been beyond my wildest dreams," Janine finally said.

Nancy cleared her throat as though she wanted to say something, but nothing came out.

"Are you done for today?" Janine asked.

"I am," Nancy said.

"Can I show you something?"

Nancy followed Janine downstairs, where they gathered in front of the office computer. There, Janine slipped the USB from Henry into the side of the machine.

"What is this?" Nancy asked as the first woman appeared on-screen.

"Oh, goodness. I first met Neal and Nancy about seven years ago," the woman said. "I was going through a horrible divorce and child custody battle, and my body was on the verge of collapse. Neal and Nancy's kindness was the kind of thing you read about in books. It didn't even seem real. But I can genuinely say that it saved my life."

Nancy's eyes welled up almost immediately. She drew a hand around Janine's elbow and squeezed lightly as the next woman came on screen.

"Neal was a funny guy. I can remember that," she began. "At the time, I thought maybe, I would never laugh again, you know? My body was exhausted and caved in. And I ran into Neal on my way to acupuncture — this was before Carmella began to do the acupuncture at the lodge and spa — and he cracked a joke. I don't even remember what it was he said. But I burst into laughter. They always say that laughter is the best medicine, and dammit if I didn't feel like I was floating after that."

The interviews went on as Janine's heart swelled. Nancy allowed several tears to fall before she collapsed on the office chair and draped her hand across her cheeks.

"I can't believe this," she whispered. "It's the perfect testament to all the good Neal did while he was alive."

"I wish I could have met him," Janine said. "He seems like the most extraordinary man." She paused for a moment and then added, "But there's no way he could have done any of this without you, Mom. He loved you to pieces. And I truly believe love gives us a strength we didn't know we had before."

Nancy's eyes glowed. She then dropped down and grabbed the box below the desk, the one Janine had found weeks ago. The one in which Nancy had kept the letters and the photographs. The one that was proof that Nancy had never forgotten her love for her daughter. Not really.

"Look at you," Nancy whispered as she placed the photographs out, one after another. "You were such a bright and beautiful little thing. I was mesmerized by you. Look, you wouldn't let go of that doll. Not for anything. You slept with her in your arms every single night."

Janine remembered the doll. But more than that, she remembered the day her mother had bought the doll for her. She'd been four years old and terribly alone.

"I wanted us to have a perfect life together," Nancy said then as she cornered the edge of the photo absent-mindedly. "Your father died when you were three — right in the middle of me trying to get him back. I guess I was nineteen years old, and he was twenty. It was such a horrible time. I was so void of meaning. I felt that I would never dig my way out of my sadness. And as you know, I guess, I turned to some of the worst things a mother can. Oh, but I loved you. And I wanted you to know it. I still want you to know it."

Janine's throat tightened. Slowly, she reached for the photo and placed it again on the desk before her. She then turned around and wrapped her arms around her mother and held her tightly while she shook against her.

"We've both lost so much," Nancy whispered over Janine's shoulder. "But I don't want to lose you. Never again. Not if I can help it."

"Ditto, Mom. Never again," Janine returned.

When their hug broke, Nancy swiped her fingers beneath her eyes and said, with a soft laugh, "I don't know what I did to deserve this second chance, but I won't screw it up."

"Me neither, Mom. I promise."

Chapter Twenty-Three

Janine stood at the front desk of the Katama Lodge and Wellness Spa as a middle-aged woman with dark hair stood with her credit card extended. Janine hadn't worked with her that day, and apparently, she'd just had a massage and a round of acupuncture. The woman was flushed and smiling. Janine took the credit card and asked the necessary question, which was, "Did you enjoy your stay with us?"

"Oh, I really did," the woman, whose name was Kate, said. "My brother convinced me to come over here. It's been a really hard time in recent months."

"Your brother?" Janine glanced at the name on the credit card as a shiver rushed up and down her spine. "Ah. Your brother isn't Henry, is he?"

"That's the guy!" Kate said brightly. "Of course, I'd always heard of this place. But I come from a family where you don't necessarily treat yourself. Mental and physical health kind of go off the wayside, if that makes sense."

"It does," Janine affirmed. "I kind of grew up that way

myself. It took me a long time to get to where I appreciate it more than anything else."

"That's surprising. Isn't your mother one of the owners?"

"She is," Janine said. "We just took a round-about way to get here. That's all."

"That makes sense, I think. Well. We lost my mother recently. It's not been an easy time. But—" Kate placed her hand on her shoulder and shrugged slightly. "I feel so much lighter and free. I know I'll be back."

When Kate padded out of the little foyer, Janine crossed and uncrossed her arms as her heart raced wildly. She hadn't seen Henry since the Fourth of July, but she'd thought of him frequently. It was like he raced around the back of her mind, ever present in her thoughts. Now, he had sent his sister this way. It felt like some kind of sign.

That evening, as Janine walked back toward the house, she shared with her mother and Elsa that she was going to call Henry.

"Henry, hey," she said when he answered. She was overcome with the warmth of his voice. She immediately pictured his face, a face she'd grown so accustomed to, even in the brief amount of time she had gotten to know him better. "I, um. I met your sister today."

"Did you? I hoped she would go over there." Henry paused for a moment. Something in the background sped past loudly.

"Are you out on your bike?" Janine asked.

"I am," Henry affirmed.

"Sounds busy. I hope you're careful. Not like that first time."

Henry chuckled. "I am. I'm almost finished, actually."

196

"I see." Janine felt her heart perform a tap dance across her diaphragm. "Big plans tonight?"

"I planned to do some more editing. I think the first thirty minutes of the documentary is pretty finalized, though, which sounds crazy."

"Impressive. How do you feel about it?"

"Better than I have about any project, actually. However, I don't know if the likes of Jack Potter would want to put any funds behind my project. It's built on nostalgia, you know."

Janine chuckled lightly, surprised that the mention of Jack didn't tear her in half. "He was never so focused on nostalgia."

"He's an idiot for that. Nostalgia is a powerful thing."

Janine held the silence for a moment.

"Maybe we could meet for a glass of wine?" she finally asked. "I'd love to see what you have of the documentary so far. It sounds like such a special project."

*   *   *

Janine and Henry met at a little wine bar on the edge of Edgartown a little after eight. Janine was surprised, yet again, at how handsome he was and that several women eyed her with hints of jealousy as she approached his table. Janine recognized the signs, as this was the same way women had eyed her all the way back in the early days when Jack Potter had courted her, and she'd then gotten pregnant with Maggie almost immediately.

But back then, she'd been a gold digger. And now, she was just a woman, meeting a man for a drink, at a bar by the sea.

"Hey, there," he said. He stood and hugged her for

just a split second longer than a friend might. They then dropped down in their chairs and held one another's gaze.

"My sister says the lodge was a wonderful experience," Henry said finally. "She seems totally renewed."

"Thank my mother and Carmella for that," Janine said.

Henry ordered them a bottle of wine, and they sipped slowly as he told her what elements he'd filmed in recent weeks for the documentary.

"I found a lot of footage with my mother," he said thoughtfully, his eyes cast out toward the horizon. "She looks so beautiful, so young. And in one of them, she's carrying me while we're out on this boat, and the sun is shining. I'm sure she thought, in those moments, that I would be little forever—that we would have our little family life for the rest of time."

Janine swallowed. "I remember feeling that way with my girls. They were just so little for so long. I remember the conversations about Maggie's spelling bees and Alyssa's mathematic equations. Jack didn't take much of an interest in any of that stuff, but I was so sure that they needed to have the very best of everything. And then, one day, they knew how to spell. And they knew how to do their math problems. And now, Maggie is preparing to be married, and Alyssa has graduated from Yale. It's sometimes difficult to understand if they still need me at all."

"I think it's pretty obvious that they do," Henry said softly.

Janine blushed. "They're headed back to the Vineyard already this week. They can't get enough. Nancy, I mean, my mom, has planned this whole spa day for all five of us. Me, Mom, Alyssa, Maggie, and Elsa. Carmella still won't play nice with Elsa. I still remember what you said about all of that. About what happened when they were young. I wonder if there's a way to resolve any of it."

Henry lowered his chin toward his chest. "They have to want it."

"I know. I know," Janine said.

Janine then went on to tell Henry that she'd received the divorce papers from Jack a while ago. "They feel so foreign to me. I hired a lawyer here on the island, Susan Sheridan— that woman we interviewed together, and she's helping me look through them and make sure everything's kosher. Since I was married to him for so long and helped raise the children, some funds are probably available to me."

"You deserve them," Henry said somberly. "You didn't ask for the pain he caused you."

"Yet because of all that pain, I might never have to deal with any of those Manhattan socialites again," Janine said with a shrug.

"Me neither," Henry said. "Maybe I've sworn off the whole scene."

Later, as Janine and Henry walked along the water, they both commented on how much they felt they'd changed since they'd left Manhattan for good.

"I feel like I used to have this constant voice in my head, criticizing myself," Janine explained, just as the tips of her fingers flicked against the bottom of Henry's. "I always had to try a new diet, or make sure I avoided carbs, or hit the gym, or made sure to attend some party, thrown by some woman, whose husband was important, in some way, to Jack's career. Looking back, I looked at everything as my duty. Now, I'm just disgusted with it all."

"And I was just this washed-up guy struggling in the

film industry," Henry said. "I just jumped from relationship to relationship, always complaining about my art and my projects and what it all means. Now, especially that my mother is gone, I want to take things slower. I want to think about what I really want to make and how it will make me a better person, somehow. I don't even know if that makes sense."

Janine's heart swelled. "No. It does. It really does."

The moon had strung out from beneath the clouds, just a sliver of it, and it cast a ghoulish light across Henry's eyes. For a soft, strange moment of silence, Janine thought that maybe he would lean down to kiss her. But instead, they just held the silence.

Within this moment, she felt it. Hope.

A beautiful, simmering kind of hope — something that told her good times were ahead.

Maybe even good times with Henry, if she allowed it.

But that would be a topic for another day.

"Thank you for a beautiful evening, Henry," Janine whispered. She leaned into him and allowed him to wrap his sturdy arms around her. He held her like that for a long, beautiful moment, and she listened to the sturdy pounding of his heart.

When she drew back, she said, "I can't tell you how grateful I am for you."

"Me too," he said softly. "I can't explain it. But I feel we were meant to have this second chance out here on this island. Far from anything we ever knew back in the city."

Chapter Twenty-Four

J anine watched her mother drop slices of cucumbers over her daughter's eyes as both Maggie and Alyssa stretched themselves back on massive porch chairs outside Nancy's home. Beside Maggie and Alyssa, ice cubes melted in gin and tonics, and books were propped up after long days of reading and lounging. Soft music played on the radio, and Nancy hummed along with it — a song they'd all heard a million times before yet couldn't even remember the name.

Janine's heart was full. She thought about how funny destiny worked sometimes and was forever grateful for it.

"Grandma?" This was Maggie, whose red swimsuit had created a funny tan line across her stomach.

"Yes, honey?"

"Do you recommend the cucumber treatment? You look so young!"

Nancy chuckled and eyed Janine, who leaned against the railing nearer to the water. "Actually, my only recommendation is to have a baby at sixteen. Then you actually are young when you should be much, much older."

"I guess I'm a bit late for that," Maggie said with a laugh.

"Me too. Six whole years too late," Alyssa countered.

"Shoot. Guess you'll have to do everything the proper way, then," Nancy said.

"Boring," Maggie said with a smile. "Although I have to admit, that wedding dress Greta is going to sew for me is so divine. I was blown away by the design she showed us."

"I was, too," Nancy admitted. "I've never seen anything like it."

"Wedding next summer, Mags?" Alyssa asked.

"It'll have to be here, I guess," Maggie affirmed. "The Vineyard is the perfect place for our wedding. You must remember that Ursula Pennington wedding from last Thanksgiving?"

"Absolutely insane," Alyssa said with a wry smile. "I don't think you could outdo that one."

"At least, I don't think we have to outdo the drama. It was basically called off, remember? And then, they got married at that little chapel down the road," Maggie continued.

"I can take you to that chapel," Nancy said. "It's just a quaint little place. Hard to believe celebrities had any romantic notions about it."

Alyssa and Maggie remained on their backs with their cucumbers on their eyes while Nancy and Janine arranged themselves on the steps that overlooked the glistening ocean. Elsa was nearly back from her shift at the spa, and when she arrived, they would do mud facials and light candles and laugh and talk into the night.

"I signed the papers today," Janine told her mother as her heart dropped slightly. "I just have to send them back to Manhattan, and then it's really over. All of it. My friendship with Maxine and my marriage to Jack. That chapter of my life is done for good."

Nancy splayed a hand across Janine's upper back. "There's only one way out of this pain, you know," she murmured after a long pause.

"And which way is that?"

"Forward."

"I suppose you're right."

"But we'll be there alongside you," Nancy said softly. "Every step of the way. Side-by-side. The Grimson girls. Just like the old days but better."

Janine turned her head toward her mother as her eyes welled with tears. "Do you remember that day, when I was ten or eleven, and you were in a good mood, and you let me skip school? You didn't have a job at the time, and we went out to Coney Island. We ate cotton candy for lunch, and we skipped rocks for an hour. You told me you would never love anyone more than you loved me."

Nancy allowed a single tear to fall. "And you told me the same."

Janine shifted her eyes back toward her beautiful daughters. "I made more space in my heart for them."

"I did, too," Nancy breathed.

"Part of a long line of women," Janine whispered as her voice cracked.

"How grateful I am," Nancy murmured.

"The Grimson girls."

"Till the end," Nancy finished. "To the moon and back again."

Coming next in the Katama Bay Series

Healing Tides

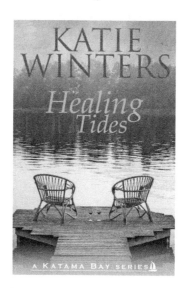

Other Books by Katie

The Vineyard Sunset Series

Sisters of Edgartown Series

Secrets of Mackinac Island Series

A Katama Bay Series

A Nantucket Sunset Series

A Mount Desert Island Series

Made in the USA
Las Vegas, NV
10 July 2024

92096722R00118